Justification By Faith Alone

In

Jesus Christ Alone

Grace Dola Balogun

Grace Religious Books Publishing & Distributors, Inc. New York

Justification by Faith Alone in Christ Alone
By Grace Dola Balogun
Copyright © 2012 Grace Dola Balogun

Grace Religious Books Publishing & Distributors, Inc. New York
Books may be ordered through booksellers or by contacting the publisher:
Grace Religious Books Publishing & Distributors, Inc. New York
213 Bennett Avenue
New York, NY 10040

Contact Author at:
www.Gracereligiousbookspublishers.com
1-646-559-2533

Soft Cover ISBN 978-0-9859713-2-8
Hard Cover ISBN 978-0-9859713-3-5
Library of Congress Control Number: 2012948732
Editing and Interior Design by CBM Christian Book Marketing
Cover Design by Lisa Hainline
Printed in the United States of America
Grace Religious Books Publishing & Distributors, Inc. New York

"He is before all things, and in him all things hold together. And he is the head of the body, the church; he is the beginning and the firstborn from among the dead, so that in everything he might have the supremacy. For God was pleased to have all his fullness dwell in him, and through him to reconcile to himself all things, whether things on earth or things in heaven, by making peace through his blood, shed on the cross" (Colossians 1:17-20).

Table of Contents

DEDICATION

I dedicate this powerful book of faith to God, the Father Almighty, through our Lord and Savior, Jesus Christ. I give thanks and adoration to God the Father for the unspeakable gift of our Lord Jesus Christ. "For God so loved the world that He gave His one and only Son, that those who believe in Him shall not perish but have eternal life" (John 3:16). God the Father's love is wide enough to embrace all the people of this world.

I Praise thy Holy name for giving us your Son as an offering, and as an atonement sacrifice for all the people of the world. I also dedicate this book to our Lord Jesus Christ for His obedience to God, the Father, in the work of redemption of the people in the world, for making it possible for us to have new life in Him.

I also dedicate this book to all who are going to read this book, for those who decide to put their trust and faith in the Lord Jesus Christ for the repentance of sins, that they will have a new life here and with Him in Heaven.

PREFACE

"But where sin increased, grace increased all the more, so that just as sin reigned in death, so also grace might reign through righteousness to bring eternal life through Jesus Christ our Lord" (Roman 5:20-21). Sin entered the world through one man, Adam. Adam's sin was transmitted into the life stream of the people of the world, corrupting all the people thereafter. From Adam's sin, all the people born into the world are born with the impulse or natural inclination towards sin and evil. Even though we were not present nor participated in Adam's sin, Adam was the head of his descendants and his sin was imputed to them.

All are guilty before God because of their own personal sin. The Bible makes it clear that human beings inherit a moral corruption and an impulse toward sin and evil. Therefore, death entered the world through sin, and now all people are subject to death because of sin.

Justification is grounded in the work of Christ; it is through the redemption that came by Jesus Christ. No one is justified apart from the redemption of Christ. Being justified before God comes by His grace and is appropriated through faith the Jesus Christ our Lord and Savior.

Being justified by God is related to the forgiveness of our sins. Sinners are declared guilty by the law and condemned to eternal death. In Christ, by faith, we are forgiven because of Jesus Christ's atoning death and sacrifice whom therefore was raised to life by God the Father. Through Him we were able to receive eternal life. Apostle Paul said: "I am not ashamed of the gospel, because it is the power of God for the salvation of everyone who believes; first for the Jew, then for the Gentle" (Romans 1:16).

Faith in Jesus Christ our Lord and Savior is what God the Father requires from all the people in the world. This is the requirement before we can be able to receive His free gift of salvation. Faith means that we believe in our Lord Jesus Christ with all our heart, mind and soul, therefore there is a response from us to trust Him and follow Him as our Lord and Savior.

In other words, faith means strongly believing and trusting in the Lord. Justification is what God the Father does for us through His Son, Jesus Christ. Justification also means the work of God in us through His Spirit. In some rare occasions, justified or justification may include sanctification, but in a general sense they are sufficiently distinguished from each other. The Scriptural notion of justification is pardon, the forgiveness of sins. It is the act of the Father, hereby, for the sake of the propitiation made by the blood of His son, Jesus Christ and he showed forth his righteousness or mercy by the remission of our past, present and future sins.

Our righteousness is not in us, but in Christ. We possess it only because we are partakers in Christ. The power of justifying which faith possess, does not lie in any wroth of works. Our justification rests on God's mercy alone and Christ's merit and faith when it laid hold of justification.

Man has always felt that he should be doing something about his own salvation, and that perhaps he might be able, through his activity, to help with his justification in the sight of God. The result is usually a growth of legalism. Some Christians laid upon themselves the necessity of conforming to the patterns of life, which they feel are appropriate to those who profess faith in Christ. This happens again and again in some churches of God.

CHAPTER ONE

INTRODUCTION

It all started from the Garden of Eden. God the Father created man in His own image, by His Spirit, with the ability to discern what is right and wrong by giving man a conscience. Human beings are capable of knowing what they have to do, therefore, applying this knowledge through their conscience to particular decisions in regards to their actions. Human beings have the ability to take action with determination in order to develop good moral virtues, which is also serves as a functional refinement of the conscience within a person.

The Biblical definition of "conscience" can be understood as one's past thoughts, words and actions for the purpose of ascertaining their conformity or deformity with or from the moral law. The conscience is primarily based on the words and actions of human beings, also known as intuition, which is a God given ability by human beings to acquire knowledge as we live on the

Earth every day. It could be seen as a spiritual thought, idea of moral qualitative mind of which is also regarded as a conscious commonality between earthly knowledge and the heavenly spiritual knowledge and understanding. It is the third out of the three stages of higher knowledge, which is after imagination and inspiration. It is characterized as a complete experience of life and it is where we can have union with God. God gave us intuition when we are created for meditation and for the Holy Spirit's illumination during our meditation to the Lord.

Communion

It is maintaining close relationship with our Lord and Savior as well as close relationship with our fellow Christians. Communion also means fellowship, whereby we go to church and worship our Lord together. This is our Lord's commandment at the Last Supper before His crucifixion and ascension. Communion is also where we associate and maintain good relationships according to the Christians belief, which was established by our Lord Jesus Christ. This relationship is generally extended not only to those Christians on Earth, but also to those who are in Heaven because the body of Christ in Heaven and the body of Christ on Earth are one.

Soul

Soul pertains to the mind, emotions and will – The Soul is the innermost part of human being that has the greatest value, especially in regards to the connection with God's image. The soul signifies primarily with the spiritual life of human being. The Bible says the human souls will be judged by Jesus Christ when He returns to Earth. Souls of those who die without repentance of their sins or those who rejected the free gift of grace of God, will end in Lake of Fire (Hell).

The mind is the most delicate work of God in human beings; it enables our consciousness, our thinking, our reasoning, our perception and our judgment. It is the main characteristic of everyone on Earth.

While emotions are the bodily experience of the mind, which is associated with our mood, temperament, our personality, disposition and motivation. Motivations direct and energize our behavior, while emotions provide the affective component of motivation, either positive or negative. Emotions are also connected with our physiological, cognitive and behavioral components, which can affect our nervous system. This has to do with our feeling and our thinking sometimes when we are fearful about a threat or sickness.

Will

Biblically the will God allowed human beings to choose, it also implies that individuals can will and make their own choices in spiritual realms. God has freely chosen to associate man with the work of His grace as a loving Father, but individual human beings have a free will to act according to God's grace. That decision depends on a man or women's willingness to accept the gift of God's Grace according to their own free will.

Body

The body consists of a physical body that developed from the stage of a child into adulthood. Our physical body allows us to move around and interact with things in this physical world. Our body and senses translate everything we touch, see, hear taste or smell into an electrical impulse that can be perceived by other areas of our bodies. While, other parts of our body are energized by these impulses that circulate through our body. The energy body is the template around which the physical body grows. Whereby our mental body is a home of the intellectual mind, which are the thoughts, created and transmitted into the environment, or receive and interpret with others such as the physical brain, which is the source of our intellect.

Death is the end of life and the permanent termination of all biological functions that sustain a living organism. Where all known organisms experience death, bodies of living organisms begin to decompose shortly after death. Death: Biblical death can be seen in the fall of Adam and Eve as they became spiritually dead after their communion with God's spirit was broken through the fall.

Three important things that can restore a spiritually dead individual are the three stages of salvation, which is: justification by Jesus Christ's work of atonement, sanctification by the Holy spirit because sin started from humanity (Adam and Eve) therefore, humanity is not the one that can atone for the sins of humanity because it was the sin that was caused by humanity. Up until today human beings cannot hear or sense the voice of God's Spirit, except when he or she is spiritually made alive.

The Lord Jesus Christ came into the world in the form of our own humanity. He took our sins away from us on the cross for our sins. Reading this book will give a clear understanding of how justification is by faith alone and in Christ alone.

CHAPTER TWO

GOD'S WORK OF FAITH FROM THE BEGINNING OF CREATION

God's Righteous Judgment

"All who sin apart from the law will also perish apart from the law, and all who sin under the law will be judged by the law; For it is not those who hear the law are righteous in God's sight but it is those who obey the law who will be declared righteous" (Roman 2:12-13). Apostle Paul is telling us that God will make known to human race that hearing the Word of God, teaching the Word of God, preaching the Word of God avails nothing without faith and obedience to God's Word and submission to the will of God.

Obedience comes from faith. We obey because we have faith in the Lord Jesus Christ. Obedience comes from a place where we can express our love for God, the Father Almighty, through our continual expression of the love for God in our hearts; we are able to obey the Word of God as well as be the doer of the Word of God. The Israelites' disobedience and sinful actions gave the Gentiles the ability and chance occasionally to blaspheme the name of God likewise today, in our society some churches or believers allow the unbelievers to blaspheme Jesus Christ's name.

The faithfulness of God brings circumcision: "What advantage, then, is there in being a Jew, or what value is there in circumcision" (Roman 3:1)? Another Scripture is telling us: "No, a man is a Jew if he is one inwardly; and circumcision is circumcision of the heart, by the Spirit, not by the written code" (Roman 2:29). This is God's work of grace in the hearts' of Christians whereby they participate in the divine nature and become capable of living a pure life, separated from sin for God's glory. Therefore, holy living becomes the outward sign that we are under the New Covenant. The Apostle Paul explained clearly to all the people of the human race, both Gentiles and Jews, that they were in bondage of sin. He let us know that we possess a sinful nature that draws us toward sin and evil. Whereby, the result is that all are guilty and stand under God's condemnation.

God's response to this tragic situation is the offer of forgiveness, help, grace, righteousness and salvation to all through the redemptive work of Jesus Christ. All people in their natural state are sinners. Their entire being is adversely affected by sin and inclines toward conformity to the world. All are guilty of turning aside from the way of godliness to the way of selfishness, ungodliness, and wickedness. The violent condition of humanity is very deplorable because the people of the world have no fear of God before their eyes.

If people of the world have the fear of God, they would have sought reconciliation and peace; they would have avoided all form of evils in the world. The Bible says: "The fear of the Lord is the beginning of wisdom, and knowledge of the Holy one is understanding "(Prov. 9:10). The Bible is telling us that if the people in the world truly acknowledge and know who God is, they will be happy to call unto Him with everything they might be going through. They would love Him, revere Him and worship Him in everything and in all circumstances to please Him.

The Spirit of God would then bless our life in a ways we could never imagine. Blessings would be upon our churches, our friends, our families, our children, our businesses and everything that we lay our hands on would be blessed by God and the Holy Spirit. All human races are under God's condemnation. By God, in His loving kindness, through His one and only begotten Son, He offers to redeem us from our sin.

This is righteousness through faith: "But now a righteousness from God, apart from law, has been made known, to which the law and the prophets testify" (Romans 3:21). This is the biggest and most important moment in the life of all humanity. A great transition that manifests itself to the entire human race through the loving kindness of God. It shows clearly that we are in need of a Savior because of our sinfulness. What follows is that God's grace never fails. The good news of God's grace, forgiveness of our sin and our redemption is completed through Jesus Christ.

Justification by grace through faith appears with the assurance of victory over sin forever. God's redemptive activity on humanity's sin, God's loving kindness shows us how to have a good and right relationship with Him, He gave us liberty over the power of evil through salvation and the manifestation of righteousness.

The revelation of God's righteousness is by the preaching of the Gospel of God. The power of God for our salvation, accompanies all believers are constantly made the word of God alive in our life.

This righteousness from God comes to us as a free gift through our faith in Jesus Christ as our Savior. In the Bible, Paul said, "I am not ashamed of the gospel because it is the power of God for the salvation of everyone who believes: first for the Jews then for the Gentile" (Romans 1:16). God the Father offers the people in the world eternal life in Jesus Christ. God shows us this right from the Garden of Eden. God leads us through His Word, the Bible, the way to salvation, redemption and justification. God delivers us from sin and death and from any harm.

CHAPTER THREE

WHAT THE BIBLE SAYS

God revealed Himself to us through His prophets in the Old Testament when God, the Father, demonstrated His love and how He saves His people (the people of Israel). "The Lord is my light and my salvation". (Psalm 27:1). "O Lord, our Lord, how majestic is your name in all the earth" (Psalm 8:1). "My soul finds rest in God alone; my salvation comes from him" (Psalm 62:1). "On this mountain the Lord Almighty will prepare a feast of rich food for all peoples, a banquet of aged wine the best of meats and the finest of wines" (Isaiah 25:6), "but he was pierced for our transgressions he was crushed for our iniquities; the punishment that brought us peace was upon him, and by his wounds we are healed" (Isaiah 53: 6).

God revealed Himself in the New Testament as the way, the truth and the life through eternal life with God in Heaven. Jesus Christ is the only way to the Father. "Jesus answered, I am the way and the truth and the life. No one comes to the Father except through me" (John14:6). "Salvation is found in no one else, for there is no other name under heaven given to men by which we must be saved" (Acts 4:12). Salvation is provided for us by the grace of God which we received and has been given freely in Christ because of His death, burial and resurrection with the continual work of the Holy Spirit in the lives of all who put their faith in Jesus Christ. "Therefore he is able to save completely those who come to God through him, because he always lives to intercede for them" (Heb7:25). Salvation is a gift of the grace of God to all the humanity. The grace of God is offered to us by God, the Father, as a result of His grace. "From the fullness of his grace we have all received one blessing after another" (John1:16). We receive the grace of God through faith in Jesus Christ. Salvation is a personal experience by which all those who believe in God through His words receive forgiveness of sins as a free gift.

They move from spiritual death to be spiritually alive in Christ, from the power of sin to the power of God. We move from slave of sin to slave of God. We moved from the power of darkness to the power of light. We moved from dominion of Satan to dominion of God. We become a new creature; a new person with a new personality with who has a right relationship with God, the Father, and the Son and God, the Holy Spirit. We are been regenerated through the Holy Spirit. We now have the privilege to maintain a personal relationship with our Father who is in Heaven.

We are now called the children of God. Jesus Christ is our brother and we are now joint heirs with Jesus where we are now under the control of the Holy Spirit who rules our hearts, mind, spirit and soul, so that we will be able to be conformed to the image of His Son Jesus Christ our Lord and Savior.

We are now in submission to the world of God through the Holy Spirit. We are filled with the Spirit of God's power, as well as in the command of the Holy Spirit who constantly is filling us every day as we walk with the Lord. With the Spirit filling we are able to be separated from sin and sin nature, and from all the corruption that is going on in the world. We are able to look, forward to the return of our Lord and to His Kingdom; we are now able to be delivered from God's judgment that will be coming to the world at the last day.

We will be able to share in Jesus Christ's glory as well as receiving our resurrected body when our body is transformed as Christ's glorious body. We will be able to receive our reward and crown of righteousness that are prepared for those who love His appearance. "He, who has an ear, let him hear what the Spirit says to the churches. To him who overcomes, I will give the right to eat from the tree of life, which is in the paradise of God" (Rev2:7).

The redemptive work of Christ our Lord paid the full ransom for our redemption. Our Lord paid the ransom price for our sin by His precious blood. He redeemed us from our state of sin, out of which there is no other way than the work of redemption. The human race has been alienated from God; they have become slaves to sin and they were under satanic powers; they were in need of deliverance from the sinful nature and evil.

Jesus Christ paid a price with His blood to free us from the bondage of sin. His blood He shed for you and I, He gave His life for all, once for all. "Just as the Son of Man did not come to be served, but to serve, and to give his life as a ransom for many" (Matthew 20:28). The result of His redemption is that all the believers and non-believers the moment they put their faith in Christ they were redeemed by Jesus Christ and they were free from the law, free from the slavery of sin and death, therefore free from Satan's bondage.

This freedom from sin though, our Lord Jesus Christ resulted in our righteousness, love and obedience to our Lord's commands expressed by His love toward us. This freedom from sin blessed us with loving obedience and glory through believers' long suffering, "Do you not know that your body is a temple of the Holy Spirit, who is in you, whom you have received from God? You are not your own; you were bought at a price. Therefore honor God with your body" (1st Corinthians 6:19-20). "For he who was a slave when he was called by the Lord is the Lord's freedman; similarly, he who was a free man when he was called is Christ's slave you were bought at a price; do not become slaves of men" (1 Corinthians 7:22-23).

The redemptive work of Christ was foreshadowed by redemption in the Old Testament. We have to remember the great redemptive work in the Old Testament. "Therefore, say to the Israelites: I am the Lord, and I will bring you out from under the yoke of the Egyptians. I will free you from being slaves to them, and I will redeem you with an outstretched arm and with mighty acts of judgment. I will take you as my own people and I will be your God Then you will know that I am the Lord your God, who brought you out from under the yoke of the Egyptians" (Exodus 6:6-7). Deliverance of the Israelites from the slavery in Egypt, where the blood of the animal sacrifice was the price paid to atone for the sin of the people of Israel. "So Aaron came to the altar and slaughtered the calf as a sin offering for himself" (Leviticus 9:8). God instituted animal sacrifice as an ordinance whereby sinners might draw near to him in repentance and faith, therefore that they may be able to experience his forgiveness, salvation and fellowship.

This offering of the animal was an object lesson, pointing to the principle of vicarious sacrifice and substitutionary atonement. The life of the innocent animal was offered in the place of the sinful and guilty people of Israel. God declared His purpose to the children of Israel, making His covenant known at Mount Sinai. God, the Father Almighty, promised to redeem Israel from bondage; he calls them His people; He promised to be their God and their redeemer. God sees that they were helpless and in need of a deliverer because they were unable to redeem themselves from the bondage of slavery in Egypt. God knows that He is the only one who can set them free. God's love for patriarchs like Abraham still continues, even up until today for the Israelites.

God's redemption of the people of Israel from Egypt served as a great beginning of transfer of the people of Israel to Himself. The people of Israel have belonged to God from the beginning of creation and election, and redemption. This redemption of the people of Israel from bondage of slavery foreshadows the greater redemption of all the humanity through Jesus Christ's death on the cross. He shed His blood as our Passover lamb, and from the resurrection, Christ redeemed all those who believed in Him from the power of Satan and sin throughout the world. Believers now belong to Jesus; they can trust and obey Him, and they can trust in His love and His promises for His believers.

34

CHAPTER FOUR

INTERPRETION OF FAITH

"What then shall we say that Abraham, our forefather, discovered in this matter? If, in fact, Abraham was justified by works, he had something to boast about but not before God. What does the Scripture say? Abraham believed God and it was credited to him as righteousness" (Roman 4:1-3). This shows that salvation by faith is not by our deeds or keeping the law, it is not exclusive doctrine from the New Testament; it is beginning from Old Testament.

Abraham was full of faith in God. He loved God, the Father; he followed the commandment of God, for example he was ready to sacrifice his only son Isaac to Him. Abraham maintained his loyalty and his attachment to God, therefore, believing in God's promises for him and for the people in his days. "The Lord had said to Abram, Leave your country, your people and your father's household and go to the land I will show you. I will make you into a great nation and I will bless you; I will make your name great, and you will be blessings. I will bless those who bless you, and whoever curses you I will curse; and all peoples on earth will be blessed through you" (Genesis 12:1-3).

On another occasion Abraham believed God when He told him he was going to have a child in his old age, when his body was good as dead. Sarah was also in her old age, around 90-years old. Her womb was as good as dead and she was barren for many years. She thought that she was past the age of child bearing or pregnancy. "Abraham and Sarah were already old and well advanced in years, and Sarah was past the age of childbearing. So Sarah laughed to herself as she thought, after I am worn out and my master is old, will I now have this pleasure?" (Genesis 18:11-12). Upon all these negative obstacles, Abraham still believed God's promise in spite of all these aforementioned impossible circumstances. Abraham believed that God had the power to do what He had promised.

It was this illustrated faith of Abraham that was credited to him as righteousness. Abraham always responded to God's commands in perfect obedience, and he maintained his love for God till the end of his life. Therefore, Abraham's faith was credited to him as righteousness.

We have to be careful not to think that the righteousness of God or of Jesus Christ is credited or transferred to the believer.

We must also be very careful not to describe justification by stating that it comes by Christ in the Old Testament by keeping the law transferred to the believers because if it is by a transferred through the keeping of the law, then it is not the same faith of Abraham that was credited as righteousness and that will automatically in turn nullify God's promise. Whereby, it will make salvation to be as a result of merit, or work, rather than that of grace. Apostle Paul made it clear that justification and righteousness comes not through law, but through God's mercy, grace, love, and forgiveness. Abraham's faith is belief; his attachment to God, through his strong confidence and unwavering faith, his assistance in God and his promises is credited as righteousness, by the mercy and grace of God.

CHAPTER FIVE

GOD'S WORK OF JUSTIFICATION

"Therefore, since we have been justified through faith, we have peace with God through our Lord Jesus Christ. Through whom we have gained access by faith into this grace in which we now stand. And we rejoice in our sufferings, because we know that suffering produces perseverance, perseverance, character; and character, hope. And hope does not disappoint us, because God has poured out his love into our hearts by the Holy Spirit, whom he has given us." (Roman 5:1-5). We have to know that to be justified has so many meanings: to be acquitted, declared righteous in God's sight. It is directly related to God's forgiveness in Jesus Christ for all the guilty and repentant sinners who come to Jesus Christ, that are washed by His precious blood and become white as snow in His sight, as though they had never sinned at all.

Justification is the declaring a person to be just or righteous. It is a legal term signifying that they are acquitted as a fact that makes it unpalatable to many in our society. We tend to distrust legalism and therefore, we dismiss anything that resembles or a legalistic approach. Throughout the Bible, justice is a category of fundamental importance. The Bible writers made it clear that God is a God of perfect justice, truth and perfect obedience.

Today all the believers saving faith is credited and equalized to righteousness. This credit of a believer's faith has been based on the truth that God justified the wicked. Righteousness of believers is a gift of the grace of God that flows and comes from God's love and mercy. The same gift of grace makes it possible for believers through the Holy Spirit to be able to respond to Jesus Christ.

When God looks at our hearts, He sees Christ enthroned in our hearts and He sees that we have strong faith in the Lord Jesus Christ. Then now that our hearts are full of Christ's faith, God freely forgives our sins, credits our faith as righteousness and accepts us as His children. God no longer sees us in Adam; He sees us in Christ. Christ's righteousness becomes our righteousness; Christ lives His life through us.

God will also give us grace for our sanctification, " And be found in Him, not having a righteousness of my own that comes from the law, but that which is through faith in Christ the righteousness that comes from God and is by faith" (Philippians

3:9). Our faith that has been credited as righteousness; brings forgiveness of our sin; is our faith in Christ and His atoning sacrifice. Nothing else but Christ's sacrificial death on the cross serves as a ground for our reconciliation with God. "For if, when we were God's enemies, we were reconciled to him through the death of his Son, how much more, having been reconciled, shall we be saved through his life" (Roman 5:10). We were reconciled because all our transgressions are forgiven because of Christ's blood that washed away our past, present and future sins.

The faith of Abraham was a true and sincere faith that endured and that God acknowledged. Abraham believed, trusted and obeyed. He was very strong in his faith with God; Abraham maintained an unshakable faith in God and he always gave glory to God. This is the faith that was credited to Abraham for righteousness and this is the same faith that makes us a child of God through Jesus Christ our Lord. Promises of God come true by faith.

All believers in Jesus Christ are saved when they believe in Christ and in God's promises by grace. The Biblical truth of the nature of saving faith should be thoroughly acknowledged in the lives of all the believers. We are saved through faith alone, the faith that saved through faith alone. Apostle Paul says: Faith expresses itself through love. "For in Christ Jesus neither circumcision nor uncircumcision has any value. The only thing that counts is faith expressing itself through love" (Galatians 5:6).

"What good is it, my brothers, if a man claims to have faith but has no deeds? Can such faith save him?

Suppose a brother or sister is without clothes and daily food. If one of you says to him, God, I wish you well; keep warm and well fed, but does nothing about his physical needs, what good is it" (James 2:14-16)? Saving faith is a strong faith that cannot do good without expressing itself through love and obedience to God and Jesus Christ our Savior. Expressions of that love will spread and make us to be of service to other people around us. Any practicing faith that made us just trust in God for the forgiveness of our sins and does not include our truthful and genuine repentance and our commitment to Christ as our Lord and Savior is not the New Testament faith.

This type of faith is not biblical and it is not producing salvation by grace through the activity of faith that not only includes being saved from condemnation, but being saved for intimate relationship and Holy fellowship with God and a life of good works as the fruit of faith. "For we are God's workmanship, created in Christ Jesus to do good works, which God prepared in advance for us to do" (Ephesians 2:10). So therefore, if the salvation, justification and righteousness that God provided came by perfect obedience to the law, no one on Earth would be saved because no one can perfectly obey the law.

The only one that lived on this Earth that was sinless was our Lord Jesus Christ, who put on our humanity in order to save us from sin. Jesus Christ is the true Son of God, and Son of man. Since the gift of grace was received by faith salvation may be experienced by all who respond to God. God mercifully forgives their sins by impartation of divine grace. His Spirit and His power regenerated our lives and made us the children of God.

The Bible explained clearly and truthfully that we are saved and justified by faith on what Jesus Christ has done for us on the cross. In the Book of James we read, "You see that a person is justified by what he does and not by faith alone" (James 2:24). He also mentioned the Old Testament incident, "Likewise also was not Rehab the harlot justified by works, when she had received the messengers and had sent them out another way." Also we read: "For as the body without the Spirit is dead, so faith without works is dead also." James is referring to our faith after we have been saved by the grace of God. It is after we have been saved that we will have a desire to do something for the Lord.

To every human being that has a desire to do good things for the Lord, God has already made that person alive in Him by the gift of grace. James is exercising two different types of faith. He showed that one faith is a true faith that is approved and the second one is false faith that happens among many individuals who put their faith in the work they were doing instead of believing that the grace of God is free, not by works, in order that nobody should boast.

This is where the Catholic Church and Orthodox believers distinguish between the first justification by faith alone, and the second where evangelicals and protestants believe that justification is a one time achievement when God, the Father, declares us unrighteous individuals to be in right relationship with God through Christ's atonement on the cross. Justification is the only thing that describes God's action making sinners to reconcile with Him through the blood of Jesus' atoning sacrifice on the cross. There is nowhere in the Scripture that says we are save by faith and works. We are made right with God by faith through the ministry of reconciliation done by Jesus Christ.

During Jesus Christ's ministry on Earth He said, "Just as the Son of Man did not come to be served, but to serve, and to give his life as a ransom for many" (Matthew 20:28). Jesus Christ was analyzing His work of redemption. His death and resurrection has reconciled humanity, the entire race on Earth, to God. Therefore, believers and all people who believed in God, Jews and Gentiles alike, Christ provided justification for them before God.

Christ clothes us with His righteousness, and His death becomes an offering to God in our place; Christ paid it all. Therefore, justification is by faith alone. Not because of any good thing or work we have done; it is a gift of God through Christ's atonement. For all of us have sin and fall short of the glory of God. We are all justified freely by His grace through Christ's work of redemption on the cross. The emphasis here is that the righteousness that God accepts is only in Jesus Christ, which is completed on the cross. Without the shedding of the blood of Jesus, there would be no remission of sins. The blood of Jesus cleanses us from all unrighteousness; it is not works, it is the blood of Jesus that atones for the human race's sins. Jesus said, "For I tell you that unless your righteousness surpasses that of the Pharisees and the teachers of the law, you will certainly not enter the kingdom of heaven." (Matthew 5:20).

Therefore, His preaching to the people of His days was telling them that it is possible to enter the kingdom of God by way of His salvation, which He is going to offer to those who believed in Him. He was also speaking of forgiveness of sins at that time as well.

Justification is an important aspect of the Christian doctrine because it was contracted by the word of James in the Bible. Apostle Paul begins to explain justification of God from the Old Testament by showing how God dealt with the sins of the people of Israel and how God brought out the solution when He was angry with the people of Israel for their sins.

Comparing the work of the law to justification, Paul said Adam brought sin to the world, which is sin of disobedience to the commandment of God. Adam's sin brought death to the world. Jesus Christ the second Adam, bought righteousness and justification into the world. Adam's sin accounted for death and separation from God. Jesus Christ's righteousness made us alive in God and we are reconciled to God through Him.

The Bible explained the connection between justification, predestination, sanctification and glorification. Once we have been justified, we cannot be separated from the love of God, which is in Christ Jesus our Lord. Apostle Paul in his entire epistle never agrees with justification by works of the law.

According to the reformer Martin Luther: "Justification is the article where the church stands or falls" Also Wilhelm Muss a' Brake: "Justification is the soul of Christianity and the fountain head of all true comfort and sanctification. He who errs in this doctrine errs to his eternal destruction." These two early Christian reformers know that the word "justification" is one of the essential parts of the Gospel of God.

Today, some evangelical churches, as well as Baptist churches, embrace the doctrine of justification by faith alone, but some of them have swayed off the road. They missed the true meaning of "justification by faith" alone. Justification, which means "justice," the Bible says which shall see Him face to face, whom we have crucified. We shall stand in front of the throne of grace, the mercy seat, the only Judge, and the Creator of all the people in the universe. God will reveal all our knowing sin and unknown sins through God's infinite love and kindness. His Holiness and righteousness will measure His judgment according to our sin.

God's measurement of our sin is always correct and perfect and is according to His perspective. The important question is how can we stand before a righteous God on the seat of mercy? We must be justified; the grace of God, in order to be justified, we must have the righteousness which is the righteousness of God and that is in the perfect righteousness of Christ. We cannot be justified by the law of good works before God. "For in the gospel righteousness from God is revealed, a righteousness that is by faith from first to last, just as it is written: the righteous will live by faith" (Roman 1:17).

Justification deals with our past, present and future sins, which our Lord paid for at Calvary. When a sinner comes to the realization of his sin and knows clearly that he deserves the wrath of God, that he deserves death not life and that he has sinned against the Holy God and against the law of God and His commandment, he will call unto God and surrender his life to the Lord and Savior Jesus Christ. He will ask for forgiveness of his sins, after he believed that he was a sinner and came to the understanding that he needed to be saved by the precious blood of Jesus. This believing sinner will be justified and made alive in

Christ. There is no work or any sign of work, but it is the gift of God by grace, nothing else.

Justification brings us to the state of righteousness before God. Justification will remove all of our guilt after we have been forgiven of our sins. Pastors ordain ministers and all the elders of the church, the shepherds are the overseers of the flock of Christ, teachers are responsible to teach, preach, analyze from the pulpits; those who are children, the teachers must lead the people of God in the maturity of the Word of God. The shepherd must take care of the sheep in a proper manner, equipping the Saints of God. They must care for the weak Christians, the babes in Christ who are being fed with the milk, not the solid Word of God, so that they might understand.

They must build up the body of Christ by teaching the true Gospel of God. They must encourage the believers to focus on the Lord, to put Him in their hearts and to study the Word of God daily. If justification by faith alone is not preached in the church today, that means the pastors and ministers are preaching what they feel their congregation wants to hear. Therefore, they are making congregations, but they are not converting souls into the hands of our Savior.

Some protestant and evangelical churches of today believe and say that, "Roman Catholics do not believe in salvation by grace alone through faith in Jesus Christ. This is not true. Roman

Catholic churches always believe that justification is by grace alone through faith in Jesus Christ. They also believe that justification is not earned or achieved by good works or merit upon any work of sinners; justification is God's gift by grace when God declared us to be righteous on the basis of Christ's righteousness. Roman Catholic's believed that salvation is clearly based on the grace of God. Without the grace of God, we cannot be alive to do any good work.

CHAPTER SIX

WE ARE SAVED BY GRACE NOT WORKS

The infused righteousness of Christ Jesus has a simple, yet complex description: In the infused righteous, speaking of those that have accepted Christ as their Lord and Savior, the righteousness of Christ has been infused into the Christians. Christ's righteousness will be made manifest in the believer's inner most being as an inherent righteousness. On the basis of inner-most inheritance of the Christian's righteousness, God will declare the Christian a righteous person on the basis of Christ's righteousness because immediately the believer inherits the righteousness of Christ. The believer has been and is automatically clothed with Christ's righteousness.

God's grace is the infused righteousness and nothing else, for by grace we are saved, not by our work, but it is the gift of God. The Bible says that we shall share in Jesus' inheritance. The gift of Grace is the main importance of the believer's inheritance.

The imputed righteousness of Christ: In the imputed righteousness of Christ, Christ takes away our past, present and future sins at the cross. Therefore, at the cross our sins were imputed on Jesus Christ, the Lamb of God, who took away the sin of the whole world. Our sins were credited to the account of our Savior who paid for our debt of sin. The righteousness of Christ was credited to the sinner. Christ paid it all when he took our punishment on the cross. "God made him who had no sin to be sin for us, so that in him we might become the righteousness of God" (2nd Corinthians 5:21). The Scripture states that Christ actually became a sinner, for He remained the spotless Lamb of God. Christ did take our sin upon himself and God, the Father made him the object of his judgment when Christ became an offering for our sins on the cross. "This is why it was credited to him as righteousness. The words it was credited to him were written not for him alone, but also for us, to whom God will credit righteousness for us who believe in him who raised Jesus our Lord from the dead" (Romans 4:22-24).

The perfect example of the imputed righteousness of Christ can be found in the Book of Philemon when Apostle Paul was telling Philemon: "So if you consider me a partner, welcome him as you would welcome me. If he has done you any wrong or owes you anything, charge it to me" (Philemon 1:17-18). Our sins were charged to Jesus' righteousness; Christ is our sin bearer. We are sinners, we have no righteousness which can wash away our sins; we are sinners and cannot atone for our own sins.

Therefore, our sins were charged into Jesus' account and Christ's righteousness was charged to our account; we become righteous in the eyes of God. When God sees us, He sees the righteousness of Christ in us. And blesses us immediately with the gift of His grace. "For just as through the disobedience of the one man the many were made sinners, so also through the obedience of the one man the many will be made righteous" (Romans 5:19).

We have to understand that the Roman Catholic Church in Rome and all over the world believed that the doctrine of justification by faith was the beginning of the Christian movement, the Christian foundation of justification and most importantly is the root of justification. Faith is the most important ingredient; faith is the very meaning and essential for justification.

Christ's righteousness, His goodness, His holiness, His obedience to the Father, therefore His sacrificial work was imputed for us as righteousness. His is a righteousness that is not in us, but inherent for us. Jesus Christ is now forever our substitute. He put on our humanity, in order to represent us before the Father. In Christ's obedience to God's law, Christ came to Earth to fulfill the law, which was impossible for us to fulfill and constantly broken. Jesus Christ became our substitute sacrificial Lamb of God on our behalf.

Faith comes first; faith determines our salvation and faith is the regeneration. God made us alive in Him through our faith in Jesus Christ's work of redemption. Faith receives the gift of grace without faith there will be no gift of grace. Faith in the finished work of Christ's redemptive work. "My message and my preaching were not with wise and persuasive words, but with a demonstration of the Spirit's power." "The man without the Spirit does not accept the things that come from the spirit of God for they are foolishness to him, and he cannot understand them, because they are spiritually discerned" (1st Corinthians 2:4, 14). "But because of his great love for us, God, who is rich in mercy, made us alive with Christ even when we were dead in transgressions it is by grace you have been saved" (Ephesians 2: 4-5).

Divine forgiveness

God's reconciliation of His relationship entails the removal of guilt. Therefore, to forgive the offense is synonymous. Forgiveness can be extended to nations and to individuals. God in the Old Testament was attributed to be merciful, slow to wrath and abounding in love and full of mercy, compassion and graciousness. "And he passed in front of Moses, proclaiming, The Lord, the Lord, the compassionate and gracious God, slow to anger, abounding in love and faithfulness, maintaining love to thousands and forgiving wickedness, rebellion and sin. Yet he does not leave the guilty unpunished; he punishes the children and their children for the sin of the fathers to the third and fourth generation" (Exodus 34: 6-8).

God's character is both merciful and righteous: God forgives and repents of punishing Israel. On one occasion God forgave a nation besides Israel and he did not bring the punishment on it as he had planned. God, as a righteous judge, was compelled to bring judgment on Nineveh, but God was merciful to them and sent Jonah to warn the city of the impending judgment. The Ninevites, including the King, believed and repented of their sin, the evils perpetrated in their country and violent ways. This made God to be merciful from the judgment that He had planned to bring on the city of Nineveh.

This shows clearly how God deals with nations and individuals. The people of Israel were distinguished from other people in other nations as being chosen by God out of all other nations of the Earth. He chose the people of Israel as His own special people and His own special possession. "Put limits for the people around the mountain and tell them, be careful that you do not go up the mountain or touch the foot of it. Whoever touches the mountain shall surely be put to death" (Exodus 19:12)/ In spite of the people of Israel's disobedience, after God's punishment of the nation, God still committed to dealing mercifully with the Israel because of His covenant he made with Abraham.

The children of God and the Israelites were supposed to enter into a covenant with God as well. On Mount Sinai the people agreed to do everything that was written in the covenant. "Moses then took the blood, sprinkled it on the people and said, This is the blood of the covenant that the Lord has made with you in accordance with all these words" (Exodus 24:8). God made unconditional promises to Abraham and his descendants, but God's righteousness demanded obedience as the condition for the realization of His promises for each generation.

John the Baptist offered eschatological forgiveness to the nation of Israel, on one condition, that they must repent for forgiveness of sin. "And so John came, baptizing in the desert region and preaching a baptism of repentance for the forgiveness of sins" (Mark 1:4). Also "He went into all the country around the Jordan, preaching a baptism of repentance for the forgiveness of sins" (Luke 3:3). Jesus Christ proclaimed the Kingdom of God and offered his followers and those who believed in Him with the possibility of eternal life. Christ was the mediator of a new covenant of salvation. Our Lord offered the Kingdom to all people on the condition of repentance from sin.

CHAPTER SEVEN

WORK OF GOD IN REDEMPTION

"Far be it from you to do such a thing to kill the righteous with the wicked, treating the righteous and the wicked alike. Far be it from you. Will not the judge of all the earth do right?" (Genesis 18:25) God can be trusted and we can believe in Him that in any situation he acts accordingly and brings justice to pass without giving any special preference to the rich or to the poor, as well as those who are in a high position in society.

The Bible says: "The Lord takes his place in court; he rises to judge the people. The Lord enters into judgment against the elders and leaders of his people; it is you who have ruined my vineyard the plunder from the poor is in your houses" (Isaiah 3:13-14). Over and over in the Old Testament, the punishment of evil is put in legal terms. The Lord, as Judge, judges the Israelite's sin and brought it out with the use of legal imagery. Many people ask the same question: "How can sinners are justified before a Holy

God? Justification means acquitted. In religion it points to the process whereby a person is declared to be in a right standing before God.

The believer should be an upright and good citizen, but justification does not point to qualities, rather it points to the content of sanctification. Justification points to the acquittal of one who is tried before God. In the Old Testament and New Testament, the question receives a good deal of attention and in the Old Testament and New Testament it is clear that people cannot bring about their justification by their own efforts, or good works. For example in the Book of Job: "Now that I have prepared my case I know I will be vindicated" (Job 13:18). Justification is connected with righteousness. During the early church in the First Century, it is clear that all the words with justification were concerned with conformity to a standard of right. In the Holy Bible, righteousness is based on a legal term. The law of God was very significant that righteousness signified conformity to the law of God. We might not find the doctrine of faith in the Old Testament, but there was teaching, which agrees with justification by faith, which was taken into doctrine. It is quite clear that sin is in the universe, but God but provides forgiveness.

"All have turned aside, they have together become corrupt; there is no one who does good, not even one" (Psalm 14:3). "If you O Lord kept a record of sins, O Lord, who could stand? But with you there is forgiveness, therefore, you are feared" (Psalm

130:3-4). "Who is a God like you, who pardons sin and forgives the transgression of the remnant of his inheritance? You do not stay angry forever, but delight to show mercy.

You will again have compassion on us; you will tread our sins underfoot and hurl all our iniquities into the depths of the sea. You will be true to Jacob, and show mercy to Abraham, as you pledged on oath to our fathers in days long ago" (Micah 7:18-20). Justification is grounded in the work of Jesus Christ' it is through the redemption that came by Jesus Christ. "And are justified freely by his grace through the redemption that came by Christ Jesus" (Roman 3:24). This verse in the Book of Romans explained two things to us (1) we are justified freely by His grace (2) through the redemption. Two great words justified and redemption.

No one is justified apart from the redemption of Christ. We are being justified before a Holy God, this comes by His gift of grace, which included faith in Jesus Christ as our Lord and Savior. Therefore, we are being justified by God for the forgiveness of our sins. As a sinner we are declared guilty by the law and we are condemned to eternal death, but our belief in Christ by faith helps us to receive forgiveness for our sins through Christ's atoning sacrifice, death and resurrection. We are given eternal life. "Therefore, since we have been justified through faith, we have peace with God through our Lord Jesus Christ, through whom we have gained access by faith into this grace in which we now stand. And we rejoice in the hope of the glory of God's" (Roman 5:1-2).

Our rewards and benefits of justification through faith are mentioned here, which is peace with God, grace, hope, assurance, perseverance, the love of God, the Holy Spirit, salvation from the wrath of God, the ministry of reconciliation to God, salvation by the life and presence of Jesus and joy in God. Christ as our hope of glory we can rejoice in all our earthly sufferings because we are redeemed for every good work in Christ. We might go through all trials and tribulations, persecutions and many various afflictions that we might be going through as a Christian – as a child of living God, we always triumph.

It might even include financial pressures or problems, our physical needs, circumstances, sorrow, sickness, rejection, mistreatment or loneliness; in all these things God's grace always abounds more, and more. The grace of God helps us to look and focus on Jesus more diligently and it produces in us a persevering spirit and a Christian character that helps us to overcome all these trials in our lives.

We become a well-matured Christians with hope in our Savior and Lord. God's grace also allows us to look beyond our present problems to a fervent hope in the Lord, Jesus Christ. and hope that our Lord will come to establish His kingdom of righteousness and godliness in the new Heaven and in the Earth. "Brothers, we do not want you to be ignorant about those who fall asleep, or to grieve like the rest of men, who have no hope" (1st Thessalonians 4:13). At present, God our Father in heaven continues to pour out His love into our hearts by the Holy Spirit, the comforter, to comfort us in our trials and bring Christ's presence close to us.

CHAPTER EIGHT

ABRAHAM'S FAITH CREDITED FOR RIGHTEOUSNESS

This truth was revealed and expressed in the life of Abraham. "Will not the judge of all the earth do right? (Genesis 18:25) God can be trusted and we can believe in Him that in any situation He act accordingly and will bring justice to pass without giving any special preference to the rich or to the poor, as well as those who are in a high position in society. The Bible says "The Lord take His place in court; he arises to judge His people. The Lord enters into judgment against the elders and leaders of His church and His people (Isaiah 3: 13-14). Over and over in the Old Testament, the punishment of evil is put in legal terms (Exodus 6, 7:4). The Lord judges the Israelite's sin, and brought it out with the use of legal imagery (Mac 6:1-2). Many people ask the same question: "How can sinners be justified before a Holy God? Justification is a legal term meaning "acquitted." In religion it points to the process whereby a person is declared to be in a right standing before God.   The believer should be an upright and good citizen, but justification does not point to qualities, rather it points to the content of sanctification.

Justification points to the acquittal of one who is tried before God. Throughout the Old Testament and New Testament, the question receives a good deal of attention. It is clear that people cannot bring about their justification by their own efforts, or good work. For example in the Book of Job: "Now that I have prepared my case, I know I will be vindicated" (Job 13:18). Justification is connected with righteousness. During the early church in the First Century it is clear that all the words with justification were concerned with conformity to a standard of right. In the Holy Bible righteousness is based on a legal term.

The law of God was very significant in that righteousness signified conformity to the law of God. We might not find the doctrine of faith or justification in the Old Testament, but there were teachings that agree with justification by faith, which were taken into doctrine. It is quite clear that sin is in the universe, but God provides forgiveness. "All the people in the world have turned away from God, all have corrupt mind, there is no one who does good, not even one" (Psalm 14:3). "If you, O Lord, kept a record of sins, O Lord, who could stand? But with you there is forgiveness" (Psalm 130:3-4). Prophet Micah's prophesied and emphasized that God is God, "Who pardons sin and forgives the transgression of the remnant of His in heritance and that he delights to show mercy" (Micah7:18-20).

Abraham's faith

Abraham did not receive the promise through obeying the law that he would be the heir, off-spring of the world, it was through the righteousness that comes by faith. Because if those who by law are the off-spring of faith, will have no value and the promise of God will have no value due to the fact that the wrath is the result of the law, and where there is no law, there will be no remission of sins. "Therefore, the promise comes by faith, so that it may be by grace and may be guaranteed to all Abraham's offspring - not only to those who are of the law but also to those who are of the faith of Abraham. He is the father of us all" (Romans 4:16). It is clear and Biblically explained and analyzed that salvation by grace through the activity of faith includes, not only being saved from condemnation of God's wrath; it is also, says that we are saved in order to have intimate relationship and holy fellowship with Jesus Christ, as well as to live a life of good works, which is the fruits that comes by grace (Ephesians 2:10).

Salvation, Justification and righteousness that our Lord provides come by perfect obedience to the law; no one can be saved by obeying the law perfectly, and no one can fully obey all the law requirements. Therefore, salvation comes as a gift of grace received by faith, salvation is experienced as we respond to our

Lord and Savior; God in, His mercy and loving kindness, forgives our sins and imparts us with divine grace; it is the Holy Spirit's power to regenerate our lives and make us God's faithful children.

CHAPTER NINE

CHRIST'S OBEDIENCE TO THE FATHER

Justification is grounded in the work of Jesus Christ. It is through the redemption that came by Jesus Christ "and are justified freely by his grace through the redemption that came by Christ Jesus" (Roman 3:24). Apostle Paul explained these two principles to us. One, we are justified freely by His grace. Two, we are justified as well through the redemption of Jesus Christ's work on the cross. No one is justified apart from the redemptive work of Christ. We are being justified before a Holy God comes by His gift of grace, which included by faith in Jesus Christ who is our Lord and Savior. Therefore, our being justified by God and receive a connection again with Him through the forgiveness of our sins.

As a sinner we are declared guilty by the law and we are condemned to eternal death, but our belief in Christ by faith helps us to receive forgiveness for our sins. Through Christ's atoning sacrifice, death and resurrection, we are given eternal life. "Therefore, since we have been justified through faith, we have peace with God through our Lord Jesus Christ, through whom we have gained access by faith into this grace in which we now stand. And we rejoice in the hope of the glory of God" (Roman 5:12). Our rewards and benefits of justification through faith are mentioned here. They are peace with God, grace, hope, assurance, perseverance, the love of God, the Holy spirit, salvation from the wrath of God, the ministry of reconciliation to God, salvation by the life and presence of Jesus and joy in God.

Christ, our hope of glory, we can rejoice in all our earthly sufferings because we are redeemed for every good in Christ. We might go through all trials and tribulations, persecutions and many various afflictions that we might experience as a Christian and a child of the living God, but we always triumph. It might even include financial pressures or problems, our physical needs, circumstances sorrow, sickness, rejection, mistreatment or loneliness; in all these things God's grace will always abound more, and more.

The grace of God helps us to look and focus on Jesus more diligently and it produces in us a persevering spirit and a Christian character that helps us to overcome all these trials in our lives. We become a well-matured Christian with hope in our Savior, the Lord. God's grace also allows us to look beyond our present problems to a fervent hope in the Lord Jesus Christ and hope that our Lord will come to establish His kingdom of righteousness and godliness in the new Heaven and in the new Earth. "Brother, we do not want you to be ignorant about those who fall asleep, or to grieve like the rest of men, who have no hope" (1st Thessalonians 4:13).

At present God our Father in heaven continues to pour out His love into our hearts by the Holy Spirit, the comforter, to comfort us in our trials and bring Christ's presence close to us. "And I will ask the Father, and he will give you another Counselor to be with you forever the Spirit of truth. The world cannot accept him, because it neither sees him nor knows him. But you know him, for he lives with you and will be in you. I will not leave you as orphans. I will come to you before long, the world will not see me anymore, but you will see me. Because I live, you also will live. On that day you will realize that I am in my Father, and you are in me, and I am in you. Whoever has my commands and obeys them, he is the one who loves me. He who loves me will be loved by my Father, and I too will love him and show myself to him" (John 14:16-23).

From the divine teaching of the Gospel, comes salvation, a call time and a command time; there is an invitation. Salvation is then a comprehensive one that comprises all what Christ came to the Earth to do for humanity. Salvation is based upon a fact about man and a fact about God. A fact of man's needs concerning his sinful nature; all men need the salvation of God, which can only be received by faith in Jesus Christ. This fundamental fact of faith appropriating the condition of salvation is also   sounds as force in some terms such as to take Christ's yoke: To come to Him, to confess him before men; to follow Him: These are all expressions of faith, the decision of faith. It is in the right relation to Christ as our personal mediator of salvation.

This means to believe in His words is to believe in Him. Because the Gospel is not something distinct from Christ and it is not different from Him. Christ is the Gospel of God; He is the salvation of God. Wherefore, faith is the ultimate requisite for the experience of salvation, and the condition, the only condition of forgiveness; it is a faith in the love of God who through Christ has brought or wrought for man such a good work.

Faith is therefore, an accompaniment of repentance. There is nothing we can procure for God's salvation. The primary condition is repentance. It is an inward decision to willing freely turn from sin to God; it is a life shaking and soul shattering inward decision. Repentance then means a change of heart from evil to good. It is a turning around from the way of sin and death and enters into the life of participation in the Kingdom of God. And this can only be accomplished by faith.

Faith is either God or Christ, or faith in the promise of God or of Christ; there is no difference. All through God is seen as acting in and through Jesus Christ unto salvation. Christ reveals to men the immeasurable love and the forgiving grace of the Father. Christ is the true nature of God as pardoning love. Christ manifested the Father like heart of God and by Him was sent to be our Savior. In the beginning, the manifestation of God as the Creator of Heaven and Earth; therefore, God the creator of all nations is known as the vehicle of His grace. During the days of the earthly ministry of Christ, He was the one that became the manifestation of God as the Redeemer of sinners.

The first can be designated the time of the revelation of God the Father as creator, and the second as that of the revelation of the Son as the Redeemer. At the present age preeminence of the Holy Spirit is as the sanctifier. From the Christian point of view, the presence of the Holy Spirit is the new era in world history as well as the Christian experience; before then, the Spirit was not yet given in the Old Testament in such a manner. This fact gave us broad characterization and it must not be interpreted that there are three successive manifestations of a single being. They are the Father, then as the Son and now as the Holy Spirit.

Whereas in the Old Testament we read the activity of God as creator as the Father; one who is aware throughout of the presence of a divine plurality of, as well as divine word and a divine spirit. This came to light in the New Testament and brought the proper understanding of the Old Testament allusions.

<u>THE DEATH OF JESUS CHRIST</u>

The death of Jesus Christ shows the fruit of justification, the fountain and the foundation of justification in the death and resurrection of our Lord Jesus Christ that was shown clearly to the people of the world. The benefits and precious privilege that flow from justification are so tremendous, as well as quicken us to give diligence and make it assuredly a blessing. It helps us to see clearly that the fruit of the tree of life are exceedingly and amazingly precious. Therefore, our common duty and the condition of this privilege is to believe, believing in divine revelation.

The revelation of Abraham concerning Christ coming and the revelation that Christ has already come. We are to believe on Him that raises Christ from the dead. Believe on His power and depend upon His grace. Justification takes away all our guilt, therefore removing all the obstacles, barriers and blockages, we are able to experience the peace of God that surpasses all understanding; the peace is made permanently. It is sin that breeds argument and confusion in our life. We have peace with God. There is no more arguments between us and God.

By faith we depend on God's arm and His strength, we are at peace moreover, we are able to receive God's friendship and His loving kindness. Jesus Christ calls us friends if we abide in His commandments and His words abide in us. "Greater love has no one than this that he lay down his life for his friends. You are my friends if you do what I command. I no longer call you servants. Because a servant does not know his master's business. Instead, I have called you friends, for everything that I learned from my father I have made known to you" (John 15:13-15).

Jesus Christ is a great peace-maker, through Him we can be a friend and a child of God. Christ is the mediator between God and man, Christ then not only is the maker of peace, but the maintainer of our peace. Through Christ we have access by faith into the grace of God where we stand with happiness and obtain all the grace of God. It is this state of grace that God's loving kindness to us is manifest and our conformity to God's grace abounds.

It is through the state of God's loving kindness we access, we were not born to this access, not brought to this access. There is no way we can obtain it by ourselves; we were led to this access as someone who was lame, weak, wretched, blind and helpless. It was Christ who introduced and led us by the hand into this grace.

Christ is the author and finisher of our faith, which means our access is not where we are, but where we stand and where we are going. We must not relax as we have obtained everything or already attained, we must stand with perseverance, stand firmly and safely. We must stand as those that are pressing forward; we must stand as a servant, as a soldier of Christ attending to His commandments.

Faith helps move us to rejoice in the hope and in the glory of God, besides the happiness in our standing, there is happiness in our hope of the glory of God. Believers that have access by faith into the grace of God may hope for the glory of God here on Earth and after in Heaven. The grace of God begins from this Earth with the assurance of glory in such a way that those who hope for the glory of God must rejoice in God now, rejoicing also continues to Heaven.

The believer that hopes in the glory of God must also rejoice in tribulations because in our tribulation, no matter how it is, we must rejoice and be happy and continue to growing in faith and increasing. Happiness especially when the tribulations are for righteousness sake. Tribulations, comes in by a chain of causes. Tribulations strengthen our faith and work, producing the fruit of patience. It is one of the powers of grace of God working in and with us. It proves our faith and improves patience. No matter how hardened steel or iron is, when you put these substances in or on the fire, it is its always softened and ready to be shaped, molded and crafted. This is what tribulation does to the faith in believers.

Patience will then become a matter of joy, because patience does more good after tribulation. Patience in our faith sanctified and helps us to experience the love of God and the greatest experience of divine consolations. It also proves our sincerity to God and strengthens our faith, love, and focuses our mind on God. Therefore, he or she that has gone through tribulation has been proved and approved of passing the test of life and does come to be as good as silver or gold. It is a good cause, for a good shepherd Who loved the sheep and gave His life as a ransom for them.

We will not be ashamed because of our sincerity of our faith has been tested; the divine love of God will continue to be shed in our hearts. Our faith and hope will not disappoint because it is sealed with the Holy Spirit as the Spirit of love. God's love to us draws our love out to Him through the power of the Holy Spirit who shed the love of God on us immeasurably from the moment we put our faith in Christ.

FIRST AND SECOND ADAM

Paul, our beloved Apostle, explains to us the fountain and the foundation of justification in the death of the Lord Jesus Christ. This expanded the love of God, which is shed in abroad Christ's precious fruits of His death and resurrection. The communication of sin by the first Adam, the communication of righteousness by the second Adam delineates our state of character when Christ dies for our sin. The Scriptures say that we were without strength and that we were in a sad condition in all the areas of our life, unable to help ourselves out of our sad and unpleasant condition. Our salvation was waiting for us and was due to come when we are really helpless.

God's time never fails to help and save when those who are to be saved are without strength. It is the manner of God to help us when we are at the point of death. There are two reasons for this, one, to be able to experience His power, and two to be able to experience His loving kindness towards His creation. The divine help of God is never late and never fails; it's always comes at the appointed time and at the right time.

Justification and reconciliation are the precious fruits of Christ's death: We are justified by its blood and reconciled by His death, sin is pardoned; an end was made of all our iniquities and everlasting righteousness was received. Immediately upon believing in Christ, we are actually put into a state of justification and reconciliation. Our justification is ascribed to the blood of Jesus Christ because without the blood there will be no remission of sins.

Therefore, the propitiatory sacrifices, the sprinkling of blood were the important tool of sacrifice. The Lamb of God was slain and sacrificed for the sin of the whole human race, every people in the world. We are reconciled by Christ's humbleness. We are saved by Christ's exaltation. Jesus Christ laid the foundation that no one has ever laid by satisfying for sin, as a result slaying the enmity, but the living Christ has done a perfect work of redemption.

Christ communicates righteousness and life to all the true believers. He shows not only where resemblance holds, but where the communication of grace and love by Christ manifested beyond the communication of guilt and the wrath which the first Adam brought to human race. In likewise manner, because of the righteousness and obedience of Christ one, many are made righteous; the free gift of righteousness is bestowed on every one that believes. The nature of Christ's righteousness brought to us by His obedience. By Christ's obedience He brought out righteousness for us, which satisfied God's justice; the fruit is a free gift upon all people in the world.

Salvation comes to all people. Scripture says: "The Spirit and the bride say, Come And let him who hears say, Come Whoever is thirsty, let him come; and whoever wishes, let him take the free gift of the water of life" (Revelation 22:17). Jesus Christ offered salvation to all the people on Earth; whoever will may come, and take of the waters of life. This free gift is unto justification of life. It is not only a justification that freed from and death, but is it the justification that entitles to life. We have to come to the realization that the communication of grace and love of Christ goes beyond the communication of the guilt of Adam. Communication of love and grace was designed for the magnification of Christ's love and to serve as a comfort to all the believers.

The communication of grace and love of God is a gift of grace; God's goodness is of all His attributes in a special manner into His glory. We have to know that God is rather inclined to show His mercy; punishing is His strange work. God disciplines, but never punishes His children. If there was so much power and efficacy in the sin of people to condemn us, there will be much more power and efficacy in the righteousness and in the grace of Christ to justify and save us.

From Jesus Christ we receive and derive an abundance of grace, and of the gift of righteousness therefore, my fellow believers, the stream of grace and righteousness is deeper and broader than the stream of guilt. God, in Christ Jesus, forgive all our past, present, and future trespasses. By Christ's righteousness all believers are preferred to reign in life. We are by Christ and His righteousness entitled to and instated in more and greater privileges than we lost by the offense of disobedience of the first Adam.

For example, if there is a big wound and you put a plaster wider than the size of the wound, you are doing more healing than the wound. Whereever there is light, darkness disappears; with the disappearance of darkness, you will be able to see clearly all what is the in the room that is not supposed to be there; you will be able to find out how dusty is the room and how much more cleaning that needs to be done.

The greater the strength of the enemy, the greater the honor of the heroes of the conqueror. Sin reigns onto death; but grace reigns unto life, through the righteousness of our Lord Jesus Christ's power of humbleness and His efficiency forever. We can see that Paul expounded and moved the great doctrine of justification by faith and therefore, also presses the absolute necessity of sanctification and a holy life. He let us know that these two are inseparable fruit of justification by faith. Jesus Christ is made a God unto human soul's righteousness, and He is made also, of God, unto human soul's sanctification.

CHAPTER TEN

PEACE WITH GOD

"We have peace with God through our Lord Jesus Christ, through whom we have gained access by faith into this grace in which we now stand"(Romans 5:1b-2a). "Nevertheless, I will bring health and healing to it; I will heal my people and will let them enjoy abundant peace and security" (Jeremiah 3:6). Prophet Jeremiah offered the people of Israel the hope of true peace in the Lord.

The Peace of God is more than relief from war, conflict, stress, or violence. It means that the believer will live a positive life of good harmony, wholeness, with soundness of mind in the shadow of the Almighty God, maintaining well-being and great success in all the areas of life. Peace of God can also spread to all nations; whereby, nations will have good trade relationship with each other. It can also result in settling disputes between or inside the nation. Nations could be enjoying plenty of wealth that they would not have time for fighting.

Believers will enjoy and experience peace inside and within the relative or within the church, with friends as well as his or her place of work. Believers will be free from worrying, anxiety and fear. Believers' feel and experience peace within one's own soul and with God. As the songwriter says, "It is well, it is well with my soul."

When God created the heavens and the Earth, he created a world at peace. Total well-being of creation is reflected in the, "God saw all that he had made, and it was very good" (Genesis 1:31). When Adam and Eve listened to the voice of the serpent and ate from the forbidden fruit, their disobedience introduced sin and disrupted creation's original harmony and plan. For the first time Adam and Eve experienced guilt and shame in the presence of God, and as a result they loss their inner peace. Before they ate the fruit they maintained intimate relationship and fellowship with God in the garden daily. After they ate the fruit, they hid from the Lord God among the tree. Instead of their daily devotion looking forward to talking and walk with God in the garden, they were afraid to stand in the presence of God.

The result of Adam and Eve's disobedience brought destruction of peace and good harmony for humanity and the entire people in the world. God has planned to restore peace back to the human race by way of the redemptive work of Jesus Christ. In the Old Testament, "For to us a child is born, to us a son is given, and the government will be on his shoulders, and he will be called Wonderful counselor Mighty God, Everlasting Father, Prince of Peace" (Isaiah 9:6). Therefore, at Jesus birth, the Angels proclaimed that God's peace had now come to the world.

Knowing that Jesus Christ came as the Prince of Peace does not give us the assurance that peace will automatically become part of believers' lives. In order to experience peace, believers' must be united with Jesus Christ with strong faith. People of this world must believe in the Lord Jesus Christ, when they do, they are justified through faith and they will have peace with God.

Believers' must also walk in obedience to that which the Lord Jesus Christ commands in order to live in peace and for the Lord of God in Jesus Christ to rule their heart and mind. Most importantly, we must do our best to live in peace with other people in the world. The early church people believed that justification was the work of God, the Father. This moved us to the righteousness of God and saved us from the wrath of God. Many early Christians from the early church have so many problems of agreement that says justification is the work of God the Father, through His Son Jesus Christ. Many early Christians from the early church have so many problems of agreement that says justification is the work of God the Father, through His Son Jesus Christ. The death of Jesus with justification clearly explained the power of the cross. Immediately after conversion there is something that is continuous in the life of a believer in Jesus Christ. They have questions as well, such as to know if justification can be lost.

In other words, they want to know if at one point they lose the gift of grace that God gave them. They also worry about the difference between justification and sanctification. They want to know if the process of sinner's sins, and when the Holy Spirit lives in their hearts and enables them or makes them alive to live a life that is pleasing to God.

For example, the apostle concept of justification was nothing to Christian's persecution and martyr. John Chrysostom, Augustine, Pelagius all believed that a person is righteous through the exertion of a person's free will to give their life to Jesus. Whereby, Pelagius' Book Commentary gives the assurance of justification by faith alone. While, Augustine taught that we are justified by God as a work of His grace, believed that our works could be used as a basis for our justification. This let Pope Innocent I to condemn Pelagius because Pope Innocent I believed Augustine's wrong assertion. Whereby, Pope Innocent I successor, Pope Zosimus Council of Carthage in the year 418 renounced this and gave Pelagius the approval. Up until today this confusion is still going on within the Catholic Church, which will be finally clear when our Lord Jesus Christ returns to Earth.

Justification by faith alone is the most important issue between the Roman Catholic, Evangelical Protestants, Baptist and others; it is the center issue of the Gospel of God, up to the point that the Catholic Church placed a curse of anathema on anyone who would believe in justification by faith alone because they did not want to take time to read the Bible thoroughly. They might have seen that we do not do any work, no single work to justify the gift of grace from God.

Our righteousness is a filthy rag in the eyes of God, we cannot save ourselves on the cross until our salvation is completed. The work of redemption or the redemptive word of Christ is completed on the cross. We can never be justified in our own righteousness, only in Christ's righteousness, when God sees us, He sees us in Christ because Christ clothes us with His righteousness.

"Peace I leave with you, my peace I give you; I do not give to you as the world gives. Do not let your heart be troubled and do not be afraid" (John 14:27). Peace is the sign of holy character in the lives of believers. "Let the peace of Christ rule in your hearts, since as members of one body you were called to peace and be thankful" (Colossians 3:15). We must continually be seeking the peace of God in our life. When this happens our thoughts, words, deeds and motivations will be influenced and controlled by Jesus Christ.

CHAPTER ELEVEN

FAITH WITHOUT WORKS IS DEAD

Both faith and works are very important in the life of a believer (James 2:14-17). For example, we put our faith in the public transportation that it will take us to where we want to go. We enter the bus and sit down. The operation of the bus must drive the bus in order for us to get to our destination. We therefore, have faith that the driver will drive the bus; otherwise, we will just sit there without going anywhere. Another example of faith with works is that we enter the ship from one country to another without the sailor's direction of the ship; without the right route we will not be able to get to our destination. The ship would be roaming around the sea or just stay on the seashore without the right direction. This is how our faith and works are glued together.

We must produce good fruit after we have been justified by faith and have peace with God. We must let our light shine so that people of this world, especially non- believers, will know that we are a child of God. "What good is it, my brothers, if a man claims to have faith but has no deeds? Can such faith save him? Suppose a brother or sister is without clothes and daily food. If one of you says to him, God, I wish you well; keep warm and well fed, but does nothing about his physical needs, what good is it? In the same way, faith by itself, if it is not accompanied by action, is dead" (James 2:14-17). Anyone who has been justified by faith must be able to show signs of a faith in God, therefore his or her deeds should be different from unbelievers. There must be a change through our actions and through our behavior. There should be a dynamic and powerful sign in our attitudes, otherwise, the person has not been totally justified by faith.

Another example

There was a man who always steals something in the neighborhood convenience store. Every time he entered the store the security guard, including the store owner would be alert and watching his every move because they know that he will steal something before he leaves the store. One incident happened that he went to a big department store and stole something; he was sentenced to six months in prison. While he was in prison, a minister visited the prison and ministered to him about Christ. He accepted Christ, and began a new life. When he completed his jail term and was released, he came back home. When he entered the neighborhood convenience store, everyone was running around and alert, watching him. He told them that they should not do that anymore, or fear that he is going to steal anything. He said, "I am a new man in Christ Jesus; Jesus has forgiven all my sin and I have been justified by faith. I will never steal a pin from your store again and if I pick up anything I will pay for it." Everybody was surprised to hear that, including the people that were in the store buying something. Everybody was clapping hands for him and very happy for his new life. He picked up what he wanted, went to the cashier and paid for it. What happened was that the man applied works to his faith. His behavior and attitude was changed. He became someone that people could trust, as well as someone that can make a good judgment of his character.

Our faith in God must be expressed in all what we do every time and throughout our life. God our Father in Heaven demonstrated His faith by sending His one and only begotten Son to redeem us from our past, present and future sins; He also died for us on the cross of Calvary, so that we may live and serve Him forever. We must be able to exercise our faith in everything that we may be going through. We have to be able to apply our faith in any situation.

Another example of faith without works is dead can be seen in what we eat everyday, such as salt. We put salt in most of our food. Some of us might not realize that salt consists of two poisonous ingredients, which are sodium and chlorine. Sodium is a type of poison and inflammable if exposed to water and too much air. Chlorine is another type of poison; so much so, that ingested it can kill the person in an instant. But the wonderful work of God is that industries and manufacturing factories put these two deadly poisons together to make seasoned ingredients called salt. Salt also used as something to preserve food's decay. Without salt most food will not taste good. Salt also used in so many ways to save lives. This is a perfect example of faith and works.

Separate faith and works could be dangerous as many people will not be able to bear good fruit when separated. But together, God's love and mercy will manifest; in the life of all those who believed in God through the finished work of redemption of Jesus Christ. "This is a trustworthy saying. And I want you to stress these things, so that those who have trusted in God may be careful to devote themselves to doing what is good. These things are excellent and profitable for everyone" (Titus 3:8),

The Bible is telling us that those who believe in Jesus Christ and put their trust and faith in Him will continue to do good that people will be able to know them. People will take note of their good deeds that they were doing around the world throughout their life.

The most important thing is faith and good works that hold life together no matter what type of person we are; a President of a nation, rich or poor people on Earth, as well as, people in your neighborhood-faith and good works always manifest and reveal the character of God in us. While believers are justified by faith alone, the believer's faith alone will not work without works.

Faith and works cannot be hid; it always shows in the life of a true believer of Jesus Christ. We are saved by faith alone, but after we have been saved and living a life in Christ, our faith should produce good works such as obedience to the commandments of God. Living a Christ like character filled life to include, living a life of holiness.

We must continuously be producing good works by renouncing all the worldly lust that can contaminate our new life in Christ. We engage in helping the poor and the needy. We are given to the work of the Gospel for the enhancement of the work of the Lord on this Earth.   We must begin to tell other people about the love of God in Christ Jesus. We put on gentleness, obedience; The Holy Spirit will be able to produce all the fruit of the Spirit within us. We are made alive by faith alone; we are adopted into the family of God by faith alone, not by faith and our works. We do nothing to earn our justification; it is the free gift of grace by God the Father through God the Son by the Power of the Holy Spirit.

The words of the Bible makes this clear and precise by teaching that that we are saved, justified by faith in Christ alone on what He has done for us on the cross. On the cross our salvation is completed; on the cross we first saw the Lord, and all our sins rolled away. Jesus Christ completed the work of redemption on the cross. He is the sacrificial Lamb of God that took away the sin of all the people in the world. The gift of God is free; it is the work of God the Father who willingly showed us His love through His Son by using Him as a sacrificial Lamb for our sin. God took our wrath and placed it on His Son who died for us so that we can have life, and life everlasting in Him. The Scripture said: "That if you confess with your mouth, Jesus is Lord, and believe in your heart that God raised him from the dead, you will be saved" (Roman 10:9).

"Now faith is being sure what we hope for and certain of what we do not see. This is what the ancients were commended for. By faith we understand that the universe was formed at God's command so that what is seen was not made out of what was visible"(Hebrew 11:1-3). Just as our physical eye sight is the sense that gives us evidence of the material world, faith is the sense that gives us evidence of the invisible, spiritual world. "For our light and momentary troubles are achieving for us an eternal glory that far outweighs them all. So we fix our eyes not on what is seen, but on what is unseen. For what is seen is temporary, but what is unseen is eternal" (2nd Corinthians 4:17-18). We must be able to understand faith in a spiritual realm. The Scripture was telling us here that our physical eyesight produces the evidence of visible things that we see around us every day. Faith is the organ, which enables people to see the invisible things.

For example: when we pray and ask God for what we desire, faith is the invisible power that makes us to believe that what we ask for from the Lord, we will receive it and have it. Faith is to believe that our name has been written in the Book of the Lamb without having seen the book. Faith is what makes us enter a plane without fear of disaster and it is what makes us believe that the plane will arrive at its destination safely. Faith is always needed to live this world of unforeseen circumstances.

By faith we believed that the Scripture is the written word of God; we apply good works by reading and applying what it says to our life, which keeps us to live a life in Christ as the good the Father required of every people in this world. Faith is not to believe only, but to freely, willingly trust in God and rely on Him, putting our mind and hope in Him, maintaining a ad have a good relationship with Christ. Faith in God makes us strong in all life's troubles; Faith makes us an over comer. Faith helps us to know God through His Word; faith helps us to see God through our heart by obediently following His instructions, which he aligned or revealed in His Word from the beginning of the creation of the universe.

Faith gives and increases our understanding of this world now and the world to come. By faith we believed that God spoke the Earth into existence through His Word. In so much that the Bible says: "In the beginning God created the heavens and the earth. Now the earth was formless and empty, darkness was over the surface of the deep, and the Spirit of God was hovering over the waters. And God said, let there be light, and there was light" (Genesis 1:1-3).

The world was framed by the Word of God: "By the word of Lord were the heavens made, their starry host by the breath of His mouth. Let all the earth fear the Lord, let all the people of the world revere him. For he spoke, and it came to be; he commanded, and it stood firm" (Psalm 33:6, 8-9). By faith Abel offered to God a better sacrifice than Cain. The difference between both sacrifices is that Abel offered his sacrifice by faith to God. God showed Abel that his sacrifice was received by consuming it with fire from Heaven. Whereas, Cain's sacrifice was not by faith. It was only by the work of his doing; he did not give glory to God. Cain was angry with his brother when he did not see fire from Heaven to consume his sacrifice.

In everything we do, we must give glory to God that He did it. He makes this happen in our life, not that something we did with our own power. By faith, though Abel was dead; he still speaks. This we must know, that not all our faith on Earth will be rewarded. There are some works of faith we will be rewarded for in Heaven. Abel's blood still speaks to us today in that we must give our best to God and worship Him with holiness and singleness of heart. Offer God the best from this Earth to eternity. We must use our life to please God in everything we do, say or have done.

By faith we must see the hand of God in our business, our children, our work, our family, our relationship with our wives, husbands and in every area of our life. We must focus upon God for the answer in whatever we are going through. We must let our light shine so that people will give glory to our Father in Heaven through our Lord Jesus Christ. We must know that Jesus is the author and finisher of our faith.

Faith in Jesus Christ our Lord and Savior is what God the Father requires from humanity before we can receive His gift of salvation. Faith means we believe our Lord Jesus Christ and all our heart, mind, and soul respond to trust which makes us to follow him as our Lord and Savior. In other words, faith means strongly believing and trusting in the Lord, our risen Lord as our personal Lord, to have meaningful and maintain intimate good relationship with Him.

CHAPTER TWELVE

HOLY FAITH PRODUCES WORK

Saving grace appeared to all the people in the world, not only to the elected people from the beginning of creation. In the Book of Peter, the Apostle, "The Lord is not slow in keeping his promise, as some understand slowness. He is patient with you, not wanting anyone to perish, but everyone to come to repentance" (2nd Peter 3:9). Peter in his teaching stated that the delay of our Lord Jesus Christ's return is related to the preaching of the Gospel of the kingdom to the whole world. God wants everyone to hear the gospel in his or her own language. He does not want anyone to perish eternally. This truth does not mean that all will be saved, but all those who reject God's gift of grace and salvation will lose eternal life. Peter explained that believers must reject any ungodly passions, pleasures and values of the world and regard them as abominable, "Do not love the world or anything in the world. If anyone loves the world, the love of the Father is not in him. For everything in the world the cravings of sinful man, the lust of his eyes, and the boasting from the Father but from the world. The world and its desires pass away, but the man who does the will of God lives forever" (1st John 2:15-17).

John commanded and empowers believing Christians to live upright and godly lives as children of God while waiting expectantly for the blessed hope and appearing of our Lord Jesus Christ. Christ shed His blood on the cross in order to redeem us from all the evils, wickedness and ungodly desires that stand in the way of God's law and His holy standard of living. God wants to make us a holy people, separated from sin, and in the world he wants us to be His own special people, a peculiar people for God's own possession.

Christ who died for our sins has given us abundant grace to live victoriously and triumphantly over the power of sin, death, and evil. The Holy Spirit of God's work includes full baptism that arrived into the world on the day of Pentecost, where God in His marvelous grace supplies believers with an abundant and adequate supply of His grace and power and mercy as a result of our new birth and the fullness of the Spirit in us.

The Spirit of God impartss God's life to believers' and to all Christians who believe in Christ and surrender their lives to God through Jesus Christ our Lord. All believers must be obedient to civil and governmental authorities, obey civil laws, be a good citizens and one that loves and respects their neighbors. There is an exception, thought, that when the governmental law conflicts with our commitment to the Lord Jesus and the teaching of the Gospel of God through His Word. "Peter and the other apostles replied: We must obey God rather than men" (Act 5:29). Believers of Jesus Christ must always do what is right and justified in the sight of God.

Justification by faith alone opened the book of the Bible for Martin Luther. Habakkuk the prophet, "See, he is puffed up; his desires are not upright but the righteous will live by his faith" (Habakkuk 2:4). Habakkuk was telling us that it is the righteous who at the end will merge victoriously. The hearts of the righteous are turned to God, and they want to be God's children, they want to fellowship with Him and obey His will. The righteous must live in this Earth by faith in God.

Faith means a steadfast unwavering trust in God that His ways are right, a personal loyalty to Him as our Savior and Lord, and a moral steadfastness to follow His ways. It is the righteous who at the end of this age will emerge in a victorious way. The righteous people are contrasted with the proud and ungodly people, whose lives are not upright while the hearts of the righteous people are turned to God, and they want to be children of God, they want to have close relationship with the Lord and obey His will. Righteous people must live in the world by faith in God. This verse in the Book of Habakkuk has put light into all the Christian's hearts and in the hearts of all other people who profess faith in the world beginning from the early Christianity era.

Christians put their faith in the righteousness of Jesus Christ, "Therefore no one will be declared righteous in his sight by observing the law; rather, through the law we become conscious of sin" (Roman 3:20). We have to look back and see how the early reformed Christians twisted the use of the Biblical relationship of faith to justification.

CHAPTER THIRTEEN

NO FAITH, NO GOOD WORKS

The great gospel doctrine of Justification by faith without the works of the law was very contrary to the notions the Jews had learned, that it would hardly go down with them. The example of Abraham; Abraham was justified not by works, but by faith. Why was he so justified? Note that Abraham's faith applies to us today as well. If Abraham was justified by works, he would have been boasting yes, but before God; but he could have never earned the merit of God. The Scriptures says that Abraham's faith was counted to him for righteousness (Genesis 15:6); therefore, he had nowhere to boast, but to give glory to God. It is was purely a free gift of grace that was imputed upon him. It is mentioned in the Book of Genesis on many occasions of his act of faith concerning the promised seed and it followed upon conflict he had had with his unbelief. Abraham's faith is not the perfect faith that is required to justification, but the prevailing faith that has the upper hand over unbelief.

If Abraham had been justified by work, his reward would have been of debt, and not of grace. Abraham received a great reward, which is God. God gave Abraham Himself. This, the Lord God Himself told Abraham in Genesis 15:4-5, "I am thy exceeding great reward." When God said this to Abraham, the moment that Abraham received the gift of the grace of God. Up until today the Lord God Almighty, Father Son and Holy Spirit is an exceedingly great reward to those who call unto Him sincerely from the bottom of their heart. He always makes grace to abound more and more in the life of His people. If Abraham had merited by perfection of his obedience, it would not had been an act of the grace in God. God gave free grace in order to have all the glory. Therefore, we are able to cast ourselves whole-heartedly upon the grace of God, which is in Christ Jesus our Lord.

The faith of Abraham was counted for righteousness before his circumcision Abraham was pardoned and accepted in un-circumcision. Abraham was justified by faith in circumcision because circumcision stands as a confirmation of Abraham's faith in God and as a seal of the righteousness of faith. God was pleased to appoint a sealing ordinance, and Abraham received it as a special favor, the sign of circumcision; they are signs and seals of absolute grace and favor of God, and His conditional promises. God does in the sacraments seal to us to be to us a God, and we do therein a seal to him to be to Him a people, people of God.

The nature of circumcision is an initiation of the Old Testament. We can see it as the sign of the original sin that we were born with and which is cut off by spiritual circumcision. We can see it as an outward and an inward spiritual grace signified by a seal of righteousness of the faith. We can also see it as a seal of covenant gift of grace, especially of justification by faith. Abraham's faith is a covenant grace than has never happens to anyone before him. Therefore, Abraham was called father of many nations of those who believe; Abraham is an example, a pattern of faith as earthly parents are the example of their children. And a standing precedent of justification by faith, as the liberties of the Father's to their grandchildren. In other words, to make it more clearly, Abraham is the Father of the Jews and the Gentiles to include all Christians who believe in Christ and put their trust in Him. Therefore, God by his mighty power of race enable Abraham to believe and hope for the promise.

It is through God Himself that faith abounds applies to us. The Scriptures says, "God who quickens the dead." It is the promise of God that Abraham should be the father of many nations when he and his wife were barren. He looks unto God as a God that could do any impossible thing; a God that breathed into dry bones through prophet Ezekiel and made the dry bones alive. "Then he said to me, prophesy to these bones and say to the, Dry bones hear the word of the Lord; this is what the Sovereign Lord says to these bones: I will make breath enter you, and you will come to life. I will attach tendons to you and make flesh come upon you and cover you with skin; I will put breath in you, and you will come to life, then you will know that I am the Lord. Then he said to me, prophesy as I was commanded, And as I was prophesying, there was a noise, a rattling sound, and the bones came together, bone to bone. I looked, and tendons and flesh appeared on them and skin covered them, but there was no breath in them. Then he said to me prophesy to the breath. Prophesy, son of man, and say to it, this is what the Sovereign Lord says: Come from the four winds O breath, and breathe into these slain, that they may live. "So I prophesied as he commanded me, and breath entered them; they came on life and stood up on their vast army" (Ezekiel 37:4-10).

Abraham believed that this same God can give him a child no matter how old he becomes. The same God can bring the Gentiles, who at that time never knew about God, dead in trespasses and sins to believe in Him and to have a divine and spiritual life. God who called things which are not as though they were (Ephesians 2:1-2), we can easily see that the justification and salvation of sinners, the gentiles that had not been a people, were a gracious calling of things that had not as though they were. This expresses the sovereignty of God and His absolute power and dominion; this a mighty stay to faith when all other things fail. It is faith indeed that builds upon the all-sufficiency of God for the accomplishment of that which is impossible to anything, but all sufficiency. It is by this faith in God that we become accepted of Him.

CHAPTER FOURTEEN

THE RESULT OF GOOD WORKS

The result of good works is immeasurable and it is incomparable, as well as incomprehensible. The main importance of the good work is that believers will be fully in Christ. The Bible says: "Therefore, there is now no condemnation for those who are in Christ Jesus, because through Christ Jesus the law of the Spirit of life set me free from the law of sin and death" (Roman 8:1-2). Apostle Paul tells us that spiritual life, freedom from condemnation, victory over sin and fellowship with God come through union with Christ by the power of the indwelling of the Holy Spirit. By receiving and following the Holy Spirit, we are delivered from sin's power and are led onward to the final stage of glorification in Christ.

The result of good works is that the believer will become a new creature: "Therefore, if anyone is in Christ he is a new creation, the old has gone, the new has come" (2nd Corinthians

5:17).   Believers are completely new in Christ; he will continuously seek how to bring sinners and the lost to Christ, who is the head of the church. "You, however, are controlled not by the sinful nature but by the Spirit, if the Spirit of God lives in you. And if anyone does not have the Spirit of Christ, he does not belong to Christ. But if Christ is in you, your body is dead because of sin, ye your spirit is alive because of righteousness" (Roman 8:9-10).

All the believers from the moment of their spiritual birth and faith in Jesus Christ have the Holy Spirit living in them. The believer's body has been redeemed when Jesus came to give them life; the Spirit of Christ inside the believer is the Holy Spirit that produces good work through them. Apostle Paul said in the Book of Galatians: "I have been crucified with Christ and I no longer live, but Christ lives in me. The life I live in the body, I live by faith in the Son of God, who loved me and gave himself for me" (Galatians 2:20).   The result of good works is that the believer's relationship with Christ is a profound personal attachment and reliance on his Lord and savior. Believer's will live his or her life in an intimate union with their Lord both in His death and His resurrection. All the believers have been crucified with Christ on the cross.

They have died to the law as a means of salvation and now live through Christ, for God. They will bear more and more fruit because sin no longer has control over them. They have been crucified with Christ and they now live with him in his resurrection life. Christ and his strength lives within the believers', and Christ has become the source of all of life and the center of all their thoughts, words and deeds; the result is abundant life in Christ. The result of good works is that Christ is in the believer, living his life within the believer. Christ lives in him or her; Christ lives in the believer symbolized the Lord's Super where they break bread together and eat together at the same times in the church.

Christ in the believer is also symbolized in baptism. Believers are baptized into Christ. "For all you who were baptized into Christ have clothed yourselves with Christ" (Galatians 3:27). The result of good works is that believers have life by partaking in the divine nature of Christ, as Christ has life by partaking of the Father. Our Lord said: "Jesus said to them, I tell you the truth, unless you eat the flesh of the son of Man and drink his blood, you have no life in you. Whoever eats my flesh and drinks my blood has eternal life, and I will raise him up at the last day. For my flesh is real food and my blood is real drink. Whoever eats my flesh and drinks my blood remains in me, and I in him. Just as the living Father sent me and I live because of the Father, so the one who feeds on me will live because of me" (John 6:53-57).

The cup of blessing, which we partake at the communion table, is the blood of Christ. The bread, which we break together and eat at the communion table, is the body of Christ. Therefore, all the believers of Jesus Christ, every individual in the body of Christ lives for Him, who is the head of the church, the first born in all creations. Christ also lives for His believers forever: "After all, no one ever hated his own body, but he feeds and cares for it. Just as Christ does the church. For we are members of his body" (Ephesians 5:29-30).

The result of the good works is that the more we love God, the more we will be able to do what is pleasing in His sight. "And he died for all, that those who live should no longer live for themselves but for him who died for them and was raised again" (2nd Corinthians 5:15). Christ's omnipresence makes it possible for Him to be united with believer, and to be present in the individual believer, as perfectly and fully has the fullness of Christ with him, Christ the source of the believer's strength, purity and life; this is the result of good work.   Believers will make great changes in their life.

When we produce good works, the result is that we will want to know Him, more everyday of our life and what apostle Paul says, "I want to know Christ and the power of his resurrection and the fellowship of sharing in his sufferings, becoming like him in his death" (Philippians 3:10).   Baptism symbolizes the incorporation of the believer in Christ, whereby the Lord's Super symbolized the incorporation of Christ in the believer. The result of the good works is that the believer will feel the need of being with and among the fellow Christians, participating in prayers, meetings, child evangelism; believers will like and join and engage in evangelism outreach, witnessing to non-believers, and giving to the poor. Believers will be visiting the sick and pray for them, to include visiting the nursing homes to pray for the senior citizens.

Christians will be willingly to do their job for Christ and in Him; the result of good works is that God will be able to use individual believer as he promised. The result of good works is the blessings for all Christians now and in the future, which is full knowledge of God. Those who have made their calling and election complete with strong faith in Christ, will totally surrender to Jesus Christ's Lordship.

They will receive the power of indwelling of the Holy Spirit. Christ Spirit will dwell in the heart with infinite love and mercy, controlling directing, instructing, guiding, leading and making His will possible in the life of individual believer, so they can be able to do and continue to do good work; this what the Lord requires from those who gave their life to Him. They will not fall from grace, but they will have an abundant entrance into the everlasting Kingdom; because of their strong faith, they entered salvation, which is in the righteousness of God and Jesus Christ our Savior. Christian life is founded upon the divine grace of God through the finished work of Christ on the cross of Calvary.

Therefore, believer's are made a partaker of God's divine nature.   We produce good works through the power of the indwelling of the Holy Spirit who is our counselor, Paraclete and heavenly guest.   The result of good works is that the Holy Spirit will inspire the word as well as illuminate our mind. When this happens we take the things of Christ seriously especially things that are revealed through his indwelling power of the Holy Spirit. The result of good works is that the believer will receive the promises of God.

"And the God of all grace, who called you to his eternal glory in Christ, after you have suffered a little while, will himself restore you and make you strong, firm and steadfast" (1st Peter 5:10). The result of good works in the believer will put their hope on the good of all people in the grace that is coming to them at the revelation of Jesus Christ. It is something which inspires grace and which in turn is inspired by grace. Therefore, it is something, which is not only God's work, but also God's delight.

The Holy Spirit, which was sent from Heaven, is the Spirit of glory and which rests upon individual believers. Our sanctification is the work of the Holy Spirit. The same Spirit that moved and did a great work in the lives of the prophets in the Old Testament is the same Spirit of Christ that is given to all believers in Jesus Christ. Christ's manifestation is His total action from the moment he became flesh until the day he was taking to Heaven. The manifestation of Christ was related to human sin and the devil's power. He came to take away our sins and in doing so released the hold that Satan had upon humanity. As a result, Christ became our propitiation, which means both to cover and to reconciliate. Christ came for this and he did it, Christ is our propitiation. In Christ, God and man were reconciled and man's sin was covered by being taken away.

Christ is the advocate within and he is the advocate above. One thing we need to know clearly is that on man's side there must be faith. And this faith is a believing, a receiving and a confessing faith. On God's side there is the divine begetting, the imparting of a spiritual life from God. We are born of God; born of His Spirit. The result of good works is the reality of possessing the new life in Christ, the evidence of living in righteousness, loving the brothers, confessing Jesus as Christ as our Lord and Savior, overcoming the world, forsaking all the worldly lust, the life of sin and embrace the life of holiness, which is in Christ from this Earth to Heaven.

The result of good works is that believer will grow in life as he continues to pass through various stages of transformation as one who loves Christ. Believer's will become the same as Christ is in his life, in his nature and expression, and even his function. The result of good works is that believer will do good works for the Lord, but the work is for the Lord because the believer is one with Him. Believer's are one with Him and by being one with Him, are in Him; He is the most qualified person to work for the body of believers must become Christ to be qualified to work with Him for His body.

The result of good works is our relationship with the Lord is not only in life, Christ becomes our life and we are His. We love the Lord Jesus Christ, and He is our beloved, as we love the Lord daily we are transformed and maintain spiritual maturity that pleases Him. We will be seeking to do what is pleasing in His sight. We will become perfect, that Lord said: "For it is written: Be holy, because I am Holy" (1ˢᵗ Peter 1:16). God is holy, and what is true of God must be true of his people. Holiness carries the thought of being separated from the ungodly ways of the world and set apart for love, for service and for worship of God. The result of good works takes holiness as the goal and purpose of our election in Christ. We are made holy by the sanctifying work of the Holy Spirit.

As we work with the Lord and become one with Him, we join the Lord in one spirit and the result of our good work is immeasurable. For the rest of our life we continue to love the Lord as we continue to produce good works. As believers loved the Lord, and grow in grace and sanctification, we need to give ourselves totally to the Lord Jesus and grow in life, therefore, we advance in the divine life and love Him more and more. The result is that we will follow the Lord, pursue Him wherever he goes and focus on Him. Christ will renew us, perfect us and equip us to work with Him; we are qualified to work with the Lord as one body in Him.

CHAPTER FIFTEEN

THE FRUIT OF FAITH

Salvation: "For by grace we have been saved through faith in Jesus Christ; it is not our own doing, it is the gift of God the Father" (Ephesians 2:8).   This is Apostle Paul's doctrine of salvation. The verse shows clearly that salvation is God's doing in Jesus Christ and we discover or receive this gift of grace without any type of work for it. We see that this other chapter that speaks about grace is how God's dealings with people of the world in regards to standing before Him is a favor on His part. Salvation is a gift and sinners are justified. This is the doctrine of God's free act of mercy in giving Christ, which lies in at the root of the apostle Paul's teaching on salvation. This teaching shows Paul's understanding of one of his gospel teachings.

In the Gospel of Christ is the release in full view the hidden treasure, which the Old Testament was fragmentally shadowed, but unclear or dimly to grasp. Paul was convicted by the Holy Spirit that what was impossible to attain by the way of law; God brought it to us as His gift in Jesus Christ. Therefore, Christ becomes the Savior of human race by His love for sinners which they rebelliously canceled, but which His nature could not alter. From the beginning to the end, the Gospel of salvation bears the character of grace. It is a gift of God, so rich and royal, reasons, and left by itself, it is quite unable to comprehend.

These teachings of Paul shows that by grace the salvation of God is brought to humanity. Salvation, which is very wide comprehends, all the blessings of the Gospel as focused in the purpose of God's grace in Christ Jesus, and found later by the experience of people's faith in Christ. In the Old Testament where the Israelites gave account of their deliverance from their enemies in the Book of Exodus, we can see the word salvation was elaborated, but it does not mention deliverance from sin. Yet wherever they go, they experience of deliverance. They always know that it is the act of God.

This motivates Apostle Paul to use his deliverance and his conversion to explain the doctrine of salvation. His experience of Christ on the road to Damascus and what He has taught him and what has come to him through the divine Word of God and the illumination of the Holy Spirit of God. Paul was blessed into the riches and treasures that God made available for him in Christ. Moreover, Paul's doctrine of salvation is also related and inclusive with the death and resurrection of Jesus Christ, that if Christ did not go to the cross there will be no salvation and that salvation would have never be made possible to all men or humanity.

The central truth about Paul's doctrine was pivotal to his experience that God saves people of the world through the death and the resurrection of Jesus Christ. Christ at the cross was vicariously related to man's need and victoriously related to people's sin. That is why Paul said that his only glory was in the cross of Christ. It was the message of the cross that Paul was able to challenge all his opponents: Jew, Greek and all other people that are unbelievers during his time. Paul challenges all the ritualism of the Jewish people and the intellectualism of the Greek. It was the same message of the cross that helped Paul to be able to proclaim in prison in Rome. It was, the preaching of the Gospel of cross that he found it to be the power of God unto salvation to those who believe.

In every area and in all the aspects of the salvation is related to the cross. Paul was enlightened by the Spirit of God to see that the cross is the act of God. People see the cross as just a crucifixion to those who believed in the cross. The cross is more than the crucifixion. The crucifixion is what people of the world did to Christ on the other hand; the cross is what God did in Christ. Therefore, the cross is very important because Christ, the Son of God died there for my sin and the sin of the whole world. The prince of glory was the price of my salvation.

CHAPTER SIXTEEN

WHAT THE POST REFORMER'S TEACH & SAY ABOUT FAITH

Dwight Moody (1837-1899) writes, "Justification by faith alone based on Galatians (2:20). Sunday October 16th, 1857 saved by grace alone. I want to call your attention to the fact that we are saved by grace alone, not by works and grace. A great many people think that they can be saved by works. Others think that salvation may be attained by works and grace together. They need to have their eyes opened to see that the gift of God is free and apart from works. "For by grace are ye saved through faith and not of yourselves, it is the gift of God."

John MacArthur: "In Biblical terms, justification is a divine verdict of not guilty fully righteous. It is the reversal of God's attitude toward the sinner. Whereas he formerly condemned, he now vindicates. Although the sinner once lived under God's wrath, as a believer he or she is now under God's blessings.

Justification is more than simple pardon; pardon alone would still leave the sinner without merit before God. So then God justifies, He imputes divine righteousness to the sinners. Christ's own infinite merit thus becomes the ground on which the believer stands before God. So justification elevates the believer to a realm of full acceptance and divine privilege in Jesus Christ. Therefore because of justification, believers not only are perfectly free from any charge of guild but also have the fullness of Christ reckoned to their personal accounts. Justification according to MacArthur imputes Christ's righteousness to the sinner's account; Sanctification imparts righteousness to the sinner personally and practically. Justification takes place outside sinners and changes their standing; sanctification is internal and charges the believers state."

John Wesley (1703-1791) Sermon #150

John Wesley was a forerunner of modern religious liberalism of his days because of his extensive concern for man's salvation and his ability in the salvation relationship. Wesley believed in experiential religion as the inmost nature of things, the nature of God and man and the immutable relations between them Wesley was concerned about man, as a sinner in need of God's grace and mercy. His emphasis was on the fact that God gives us the freedom to respond in grace. Wesley's fundamental truth was the possible salvation of all men who are sinners, and Wesley believed that there is no neutrality or natural ability to respond to

God in grace, but the response was created by God himself. Right from the day of his conversion he said. "I believed justification by faith alone as much as I believe there is God. I have never varied from it, no, not an hairs breath from 1738-1766 – he stated that justification by faith is the very foundation of our church Anglican and it is the fundamental doctrine of the reformed church. But what is it to be justified" what is justification? This was the second thing, which I propose to show. And it is evident, from what has been already observed that it is not the being made actually just and righteous. This is "sanctification" which is, indeed, in some degree, the immediate fruit of justification, but nevertheless, is a distinct gift of God, and of a totally different nature."

John Calvin (1509-1564)

John Calvin – "explained justification simply as the acceptance with which God receives us into His favor as righteous men and women. And we say that it consists in the remission of sins and the imputation of Christ righteousness. Calvin taught and explained during his life time that justification by faith and the assurance that God accepts us as righteous, but this does not mean that we can just continue to sin. Justification always goes hand in hand by sanctification. As Christ cannot be turn into parts, so these two which we perceive in Him together and conjointly are inseparable namely, righteousness and sanctification. Whomever therefore, God receives into grace, on them he at the same time bestows the spirit of adoption, by whose power He remake them to his own image, therefore Christ justifies no one whom he does not at the same time sanctify. The reason they always go together is that we have them both by being united to Christ now, both repentance and forgiveness of sins that is, newness of life and free reconciliation are conferred on us by Christ and both are attained by us through faith."

Martin Luther – (1483-1546)

Martin Luther: Justification by faith alone - The reformation doctrine of justification by faith is, and has always been, the number one target of the enemy's attack. It provides the foundation of the bridge that reconciles God and man- without the key doctrine, Christianity falls. But the doctrine that the reformers so pain staking clarified, even spilled blood over has become so muddled today that many Protestants barely recognize it. Sadly, there are some who react against a clear presentation of justification, calling it nothing more than useless hair splitting. Martin Luther found the truth in the same verse he had stumbled over, "For in the gospel righteousness from God is revealed, a righteousness that is by faith from first to last, just as it is written; The righteous will live by faith" (Romans 1:17). Luther had always seen the righteousness of God as an attribute of the sovereign Lord by which he judged sinners not attributed sinners could ever possess. He described the break through that put an end to the theological dark ages. "I saw the connection between the justice of God and the statement that the just shall live by His faith." Then I grasped that the justice of God is that righteousness by which through grace and sheer mercy of God justifies us through faith. Justification by faith was the great truth that dawned on Luther and dramatically altered the church. Because Christians are justified by faith alone, their standing before God is not in any way related to personal merit. Good work and practical holiness do not provide the grounds for acceptance with God. God receives as righteous those who believe, not because of any good thing he sees in them not even because of His own sanctifying work in their lives, but solely on the basis of Christ righteousness, which is reckoned to their account."

CHAPTER SEVENTEEN

EXAMPLE OF FAITH

Apostle James said: "Faith without work is dead." "Because you know that the testing of your faith develops perseverance. Perseverance must finish its work so that you may be mature and complete, not lacking anything. If any of you lacks wisdom, he should ask God, who gives generously to all without finding fault, and it will be given to him. But when he asks, he must believe and not doubt, because he who doubts is like a wave of the sea, blown and tossed by the wind. That man should not think he will receive anything from the Lord; he is a double-minded man, unstable in all he does" (James 2:17, 1:3-7).

Many people in the world misinterpret Apostle James words about faith because they don't read the Bible or they do not have thorough knowledge of the meaning of the Biblical words. "Was not our ancestor Abraham considered righteous for what he did when he offered his son Isaac on the alter?" (James 2:21),

"Abraham believed the Lord, and he credited it to him as righteousness" (Genesis 15:6), "However, to the man who does not work but trust God who justifies the wicked, his faith is credited as righteousness" (Roman 4:5). James was giving explanation that if people are genuinely, truly saved by faith, then they will bear fruit of good works in their life that will show people around them that they are really born again Christians. "But the Lord said to Samuel, Do not consider his appearance or his height, for I have rejected him. The Lord does not look at the thing man looks at. Man looks at the outward appearance, but the Lord looks at the heart" (1st Samuel 16:7).

Christians who process the Holy Spirit is active in their heart; they have strong faith in the Lord. James' teaching emphasizes that there should be some good works in a man and woman of God, means that a devoted Christian without works is not saved. They are saved the moment they gave their life to Christ; they become a child of God through faith in Christ. The Book of James is a challenge to all the Christians, all believers, the sinners and the lost. It is the same in the Book of Matthew.

Christian access into the standing of grace is only by faith and through Jesus Christ alone. We cannot do anything that will make them stand before God. The access of grace is an introduction to His divine presence. It is a great blessing and privilege. We are in Christ, we remain in Christ, to be the adopted son of God and to be a member of His household, to be able to walk with Him in the light as he is in the Light, to behold His face the face of one and only the true Son of God full of grace and truth. The most important aspect of our standing in His grace means we will be able to rejoice in hope of the glory of God.

Many Evangelical Pastors embrace the justification by faith alone, but they are not practicing what they preach, meaning they are not preaching the truth of justification on the pulpit, their making a congregation, but they are not converting soul into the hands of the Lord. Churches of Christ must expand the teaching of Justification by faith alone through Christ alone on the pulpit. They need to expand justification and the full meaning of it in proclaiming the Gospel of God.

Believers must realize that one day they are going to be at the Judgment Seat of Christ. One day God will expose all our sins and secret sins in front of His throne. We will account for everything we have done on Earth, either good or bad. We have to know that God's judgment is never according to humanity's standard, He will judge His creature with an iron hand, and He gave us so many chances to repent from our sins. There is nothing good in human flesh and we cannot cleanse or purify ourselves and make ourselves free from sin or from any unrighteousness.

People of this world need to be justified in order to be justified, people must have a righteousness, which equals to the righteousness of and this can only be found in Christ's righteousness. Justification deals with our past present and future sins, which Christ has dealt with on the cross. On the cross, Christ washes away our past, present, and future sins away. Christ clothes us with His righteousness. Justification is far more than forgiveness of sin; justification removal of the guilt permanently from our heart.

Pastors, ministers and church leaders such as elders of the church shepherding and leading the flocks, the body of Christ from baby in Christ to a matured Christian are solely responsible for not preaching and teaching their congregation about the justification by faith. This is the reason why some churches are lukewarm, weak and full of worldly characters. Some Baptist, Evangelical and Protestant churches pointing fingers to the Roman Catholic churches saying that Roman Catholic teaches that salvation by grace and works through faith through in Jesus Christ. Whereas, Roman Catholic churches believed that justification by grace the cross of Calvary.

We must be aware that Roman Catholic Church believed that justification will not be earned by good works or any performance of our own, justification is solely based on the gift of God's grace. Justification of God by faith, declared a sinner to be righteous only on the basis of Christ's righteousness. Some Catholic Churches believed that believer's salvation is on the grace of God and it is based only on Christ's righteousness.

The Catholic Church believed that all Christian's good works and all the good life they possess is based on the grace of God, because without God's grace to humanity, we cannot do or perform any good works. For example, of Apostle Paul's message to Philemon is an example of Imputed righteousness of Christ, which means charging to another account, or making someone else accountable for the wrong that the person did, or put the blame on someone else: "So if you consider me a partner, welcome him as you would welcome me. If he has done you any wrong or owes you anything, charge it to me. I, Paul am writing this with my own hand. I will pay it back not to mention that you owe me your very self" (Philemon 1:17-19).

There is no way a sinner can re-do the damage they have done to God; there is no way they can be able to pay God back for the sins they have done against Him. Christ paid our debt because Christ is the only one that can carry all the wrath of God. We can never know how plenty, how heavy and how many is the wrath of God. God knows that Christ is the only one that can take away are past, present and future sins. Therefore, all the wrath of God, the Father, was imputed on God, the Son, Jesus Christ our Lord and Savior.

Another example: A murderer that kill someone's child says that he is sorry in court, but his sorry cannot bring the child that died back. But the sins of the murderer can be charged to the account of Christ and His righteousness will be charged to the murderer's account.

Synthetic justification has to do with something adding to another, example cotton added to polyester; when God sees the sinner, he will not find enough righteousness to declare the sinner justified. Naked we come to God, He clothe us with the righteousness of Christ. Righteousness is never inherent, but it is the gift of the grace of God added to Christ's righteousness. The addition can only possible through Christ's righteousness.

Jesus Christ is our substitute when He put on our humanity and became a man; He put on our human flesh in order to represent us before the Father while on Earth. He fulfilled all the law of God, "Do not think that I have come to abolish the Law or the Prophets: I have not come to abolish them but to fulfill them" (Matthew 5:17). The expression of the Law and the Prophets was used comprehensively in the Old Testament. Christ did not come to abolish or change the Law. Jesus Christ has no intention to abolish the law. He came to fulfill the Law, especially in the lives of those who believe in Him. Christ made this clear in His words then, and now that all those who believed in Him, must not view the law as a system of legal commandments by which to obtain merit for forgiveness and salvation. They must see the law as a moral code; this statement was for those who are already in good relationship with God by obedience, as well as those who have expressed the life of Christ within themselves. Faith in Christ is the point of departure for the fulfilling of the law. Through faith in Christ, God becomes our Father.

Christ's righteousness is not inherent; it is imputed. His goodness, His holiness, His righteousness, His obedience to the Father charged and credited to sinner's account. There is a difference between infused righteousness and the imputed righteousness, imputed is the righteousness that is inside you, and the infused is the righteousness that is outside you. The most important in this is that faith is the instrumental cause for justification.

The Father is the initial movement, the foundation of justification and the root of justification. Roman Catholic's believes that faith is essential for justification. And by the infusion of the righteousness of Christ, sinners can enter into sacraments and works. "For we are God's workmanship, created in Christ Jesus to do good works, which God prepared in advance for us to do" (Ephesians 2:10).

CHAPTER EIGHTEEN

WE LIVE BY FAITH, NOT BY SIGHT

The salvation, which is effective for us because our union is with Him. To be saved is to be united with Christ. Union with Christ is by all means salvation. Union with Christ and understanding of the intimate relationship of oneness with Christ in His death and resurrection and most importantly, understanding of God's saving grace. By this union with Christ, we are rescued by justification from being a legal fiction. Salvation is not just something for us; it is also something done in us.

To be united with Christ is to know our justification; it is to be declared righteous before God; and being united with Christ is to have our sanctification. If justification is God declaring us righteous in His sight and sanctification is God making us righteous, as it is often put in the interest of clarity and neatness, it needs to be stressed that the two cannot be separated. Both justification and sanctification are connected with our union with

Christ. God's judicial act of His loving kindness declaring us righteous is closely bound up with our death to sin. Therefore, it must be clear that "justified by faith" is to enter into a living union with Christ in order to live a Christ like justification by faith, which was apostle Paul's dynamic and creative life experience.

It is once in every human life. The new life in Christ must be unfolded. The righteousness, which God bestow is a righteousness that God looks after and approves. In Christ we know what we are; and in Christ we become what we are, or what He wants us to be for His glory. To know Jesus Christ in justification and sanctification is our through the power of the Holy Spirit. Justification opens into the new life, and sanctification develops that life in union with Christ by the Holy Spirit. This means sanctification of the Spirit, brought forward by the Holy Spirit.

In this union with Christ, "He predestined us to be adopted as his sons through Jesus Christ, in accordance with his pleasure and will" (Ephesians 1:5), we are adopted into God's family, we are a new creature and we are children of God. "You are all sons of God through faith in Christ Jesus" (Galatians 3:26). We receive our son-ship in Christ. "For you did not receive a spirit that makes you a slave again to fear, but you received the Spirit of Son ship, and by him we cry, Abba, Father" (Romans 8:15). "For it is by grace you have been saved, through faith, and this not from yourselves, it is the gift of God" (Ephesians 2:8). And finally it is the gift of grace through faith, and divine initiative of the grace of God; human response is faith in the finished work of Jesus Christ. Faith is the foundation of salvation. It is very important to be justified in the sight of God. And it is only possible through Christ.

CHAPTER NINETEEN

FAITH ALONE

Justification by faith alone stated that we are sinners and faced the wrath of God, but God send His Son to the world. Upon His account we were able to receive God's pardon, we received unto us God's unending favor, we are declared or pronounced righteous and acquitted from all our guilt of sins. He removed the curse of Adam and Eve, and turns away from His wrath towards us. God gave believers a right and blessed us with eternal life in Him. Because by one man's disobedient sin entered the world and by one man's righteousness, the righteousness of Jesus Christ alone, efficacious in the justification of us all. This is the righteousness of Christ, even His obedience, whereby in all things He fulfilled the will of His Father; as on the other hand, our unrighteousness is our disobedience and our transgression of the commandments of God.

The Bible says that through the operation of God, there is a state where the constituted and united of our soul with Christ which is different from God's natural and providential concurs us with all the believer's spirit, as well as from all union of mere association, or sympathy, moral likeness, or moral influence, union of life, in which the human spirit. While, most individual believers possess their personal distinctness, interpenetrated and energized by the spirit of Christ. The believer is made indissolubly one with Christ and becomes a member or partaker of regeneration, believing and justified humanity of which Christ is the head and the hope of glory. After we have been justified by faith and receive the gift of grace we now become one with Christ; we are now ready to add works with our faith through our union with Christ.

Therefore, we are maintaining a personal relationship with Him, the risen, the ever living, the ascended, our reserved and omnipresent Lord Jesus Christ. Our union with Christ is the central truth of the Christian doctrine for all people in the universe. Our oneness with Christ is always at the ground of regeneration and justification.

Salvation is through the redemptive work of Christ, therefore, our oneness with Jesus is planned and directed, controlled by the Holy Spirit, which renewed and justified believers. We receive Christ's atonement, God elects and call us the sinners begin in regeneration, which was completed in our conversion, declared justification and approved in sanctification with perseverance. The blessing of oneness with Christ is the justification by faith. Justification brings or changes the believer's moral character, that began or started with regeneration and is completed through sanctification. When a sinner is born again, it will show in his faith, hope in the Lord, love and he will be a living holy life. Regeneration is completed with believer's repentance, faith justification, sanctification and glorification. Most importantly, this one life with Christ makes regeneration and all others things with it a great blessings.

It is the life of Christ who joins Himself to us in order that we may join ourselves with Him and be one in Him, as he and Father are one. The Holy Spirit is the principle master planner between the believer, God the Father, and God the Son with the immeasurable power of the Holy Spirit. Christ gave Himself to those who love Him, to those who believe in Him with intimate personal relationship with Him. We see that regeneration and the work of the Holy Spirit in conversion cannot be separated. Only in Christ and through Christ a sinner becomes a new creature, justified. To be one in Christ is to begin immediately after our conversion we are one in Christ, we are regenerated and justified. Both these two are the divine side of humanity, sinners turn only as God turns him. God imparts life to man and man becomes a living being. The same happened in regeneration and conversion. If God did not makes us alive in Himself, pastors might be preaching from morning 'til night and the sinner will not turn, but as God made the sinner alive in Him, the sinner will immediately turn to God. This is the gift of the grace of God.

The majority of believers, as well as nonbelievers, always think that God is too far away from them. They don't believe that God the Son can live in their heart by His Spirit, but with the power of Christ's omnipresence and the power of the work of redemption, Christ is able to manifest His full presence in the life of the individual of those who believe in Him and with the power of the Holy Spirit, sinners were able to receive the fullness of the Spirit of Christ, which is the Spirit of God. Jesus Christ was able to be with us in every place, in everywhere, in everything we are doing and about to do, in our home, work place, and in the church. Individual believers receive the fullness of Christ and Christ became the source of strength, the source of believer's pour life; Christians were able to confidently say Christ gives us great wisdom and in Him we can do anything because He cares for His children. This oneness is the source of our stability. Once this is formed it cannot be dissoluble. There are many ties in the world that are always broken, but our oneness in Christ will endure forever, from this earth to eternity.

CHAPTER TWENTY

CHRIST ALONE

Christ, who was in the form of God, emptied himself and came to the world in obedience and humility even unto death on the cross. He has won for all people of the world complete salvation. Therefore, or moreover, the cross has never been isolated; it has never separated from the person of Jesus, or from the resurrection of Jesus after His death, burial, rise and ascension. The cross is the cross of the Son of God, which connected to the empty tomb that becomes God's instrument of the saving act of grace.

The cross and the empty tomb emphasized the uniqueness of Christ's death and resurrection, which is continuously shining on the people of the Earth up until today. Apostle Paul related the cross of Christ to God's redeeming love. There was darkness over all the Earth, which Lord Jesus Christ went through, but the cross was secured, in the eternal heart of God. The death of Christ on the cross shows us clearly the love of God for us. "For God so loved the world that he gave his one and only Son, that whoever believes in him shall not perish but have eternal life" (John 3:16). God Almighty. Father of creation, gave His Son as an offering for the sin of the whole world on the cross.

Apostle Paul and many believers today see clearly that the death of Christ as a or the supreme evidence of a divine love of God, which could not let us go; which God turned to us, when we had turned away from Him. The cross was done in the full light of God's presence, by His own begotten Son in whom the Father is well pleased. On the cross Christ bled so that He could bless. It was on the cross that Apostle Paul discovered that the condemnation and the applying power of the law were shattered. Christ became a curse for us; the cross redeems us from the curse of the law. To die on the cross was to recognized accursed. The Jews looked outside the city and saw Him who died as accursed on the tree. The law proclaimed Him to be outcast, condemned, despised and rejected of men. Christ went through all the agony for us.

The cross relates not only to the rules of the law, but also to the reality of human sin. Christ alone among all the Sons of men has ever known the meaning and the impact, and the measure of sin when He took our sins in His own body to the cross. The most astonishing face in the whole New Testament about our Lord, is that there was nothing in the entire world that could amaze the Son of God, but the huge totality of human sins. And he had it all laid upon Himself, until he was made sin. Sin is so exceeding sinful, so unspeakable, evil, that in amazement, the Son of God went down into death and Hell.

We do not know the reality of sin. Christ took the cup and let its poison to bring about His death on the cross. This is the atonement of the cross, there is salvation only by the death of Jesus. For at the cross all sin's sting has been taken by Jesus, all the sin's cup of the wrath of God was drunk by Jesus Christ our sin bearer; there was not a drop left for us to drink.

Christ Jesus drunk it all, he paid it all for our sin. On the cross, Christ did for us what we could have never done for ourselves and for anyone, he willingly gave His life for us. God's deed in Christ for us in many ways was the herald of Salvation. At an infinite cost Christ paid the price for our sin. We have been bought out to be His own forever and forever. We have been purchased by Jesus Christ; he paid for our sin in full with His precious blood on the cross. The redemptive work of Christ was completed on the cross.

Apostle Paul uses the word propitiation in an effort to make it clearer to us what Christ accomplished for us on the cross. The death of Christ made propitiation for our sin and the sin of all the people in the world. The word propitiation also revealed that there was a wrath of God against sin. To deny the wrath of God is to do or engage in violence, or to nullify the verdict of the human sense of guilt. In the cross, Christ removed the obstacles in the way of God's love flowing into the heart of people in the world.

And in the wrath of God, which was real; there also we found the love of God, which was so deep. Therefore, what the righteousness of God demanded, his loving kindness provided. And the loving righteousness of God cannot be heeding. It is God Himself who has set forth Christ's propitiation. In the cross, God's wrath is seen in judgment; as well as in the cross God's love is seen in mercy. Christ has done justice to the character of God by providing propitiation in His blood. And indeed the deed is done, then the perfect substitute is found; He has paid the ransom; the propitiation is made.

Another word that Apostle Paul used in the New Testament is that clarified justification by faith alone is the word "reconciliation." Reconciliation indicates a profound understanding of the cross. "For if, when we were God's enemies, we were reconciled to him through the death of his Son, how much more, having been reconciled, shall we be saved through his life" (Roman 5:10), "that God was reconciling the world to himself in Christ, not counting men's sins against them" (2nd Corinthians 5:19), the idea of Christ as a reconciler is a fundamental one in the Gospel of God. The word reconciling carries a healing power. Because in the teaching of Christ "reconciliation" is a divine anointed and inspiring that was the actual identification made with the sinners.

This is where Christ is mostly seen as the mediator of a New Covenant, and His performances as the ministry of reconciliation. We must be aware, that it is in the light of the cross that Christ was able to reconcile the people of God to himself, which is the goal of coming to Earth. Christ's strongest statement of work on others is the ministry of reconciliation. It is human race's hostility towards God that we find the permanent answer. Moreover, it is in the cross that God's hostility towards humanity, was conditioned by the human sin, is overcome. Because of divine necessities, which must be complete, and God's principles of justice and righteousness, which could never be set aside; the cross is the answer that satisfied principles for the wrath of God. At the cross, God Himself has made reconciliation in Christ. At the cross, God restored our relationship between Him and us in the death of Jesus Christ His Son.

"Once you were alienated from God and were enemies in your minds because of your evil behavior" (Colossians 1:21). By sin God's heart was wounded and His Holiness faded away from the evil man. For sin not only stained human life, it also strained divine love. At the cross we see infinite pain in the presence of human sin, uniting with God's boundless and all comprehensive love.

In the atoning work of Jesus Christ, God has exhibited his righteousness and expressed His condemnation of sin, therefore, He reconciled the sinner to himself by putting away sin. In that that is where and in it all, through it all, his love shined on us. We must know that the reconciling work on the cross is beyond the bringing of sinner and God together. It involved the unity of human race, bringing all the human races of the world into one at the cross. Everywhere sin divided; the cross of Christ always unites. When we are far away from God and are not living a righteous life, they tend to think evil and do evil to their men or to one another.

It is when people are in a right relationship with God they will be able to find in others good things in a community of nature and things of interest which lifts them up above prejudice and the corrosive power of suspicion. It is in Christ that God has been pleased to reconcile all the humanity to Him.

In the cross all things are reconciled. The universe, cursed with sin's curse, hostile with sin's hostility, is given new status by God's own act in Christ. And that is why the Bible says: "There is going to be a new heaven and a new earth wherein dwells righteousness" (2nd Peter 3:13). Because of the death of Christ, God has nothing against us anymore. His wrath has been appeased, and his love has found away. Those who received the reconciliation have been committed to the proclamation of the healing power of the word of God. This is the salvation, which Christ procured for us.

The redeeming work of Christ is incomprehensible; Christ offered Himself for us and now He lives to intercede on our behalf at the right hand of God the Father. Christ is known as High Priest, Christ is portrayed as our High Priest, Apostle, Mediator, Pioneer, Shepherd, Forerunner, Surety. Jesus is Son of God; Christ is the brightness of God's glory and the express image of His person. Christ is the only one whom God's glory is fully expressed and on whom God's character is perfectly bestowed, Christ whom the world was made and the universe upheld. Jesus Christ the Son of God is pre-eminence over the angels in Heaven.

The Scripture says: "Jacob left Beersheba and set, out for Haran when he reached a certain place; he stopped for the night because the sun had set. Taking one of the stones there, he put it under his head and lay down to sleep. He had a dream in which he saw a stairway resting on the earth, with its top reaching to heaven, and the angels of God were ascending and descending on it. There above it stood the Lord, and he said: "I am the Lord, the God of your Father Abraham and the God of Isaac. I will give you and your descendants the land on which you are living. Your descendants will be like the dust of the earth, and you will spread out to the west, and to the east, to the north and to the south. All peoples on earth will be blessed through you and your off-spring. I am with you and will watch over you wherever you go, and I will bring you back to this land. I will not leave you until I have done what I have promised you" (Genesis 28:10-15).

This vision of the angels suggests that they play an important role in God's protection and guidance of his people. Under the New Covenant Christ Jesus is the ladder to heaven as in the story of Jacob. Christ is the way, the truth and the life, only through him we can get to Heaven. Christ is the center of all creations. Angels and the entire heavenly host also play an active role in the lives of believers. God came to Jacob with the message that the blessing promised will be accomplished through Christ's redemptive work that reach all the people on Earth. The Book of Hebrew says: "Jesus Christ is the same yesterday and today and forever" (Hebrew 13:8). The verse is telling us the truth that Jesus Christ does not change; he provides a sure anchor for our faith. It means that believers must not be content until they experience the same salvation, communion with God, baptism in the Holy Spirit and kingdom power that the New Testament believers experienced in their service to God through Jesus Christ. Christ is distinguished from people of the world. Men and women change their mind because they cannot see or know what tomorrow will bring, but Jesus Christ, the Son of God, knows tomorrow and knows the number of our years. He is a changeless, loving, righteous and wise who responds to all the circumstances we might be going through with wisdom and power because he foreknew the circumstances. He is the all-knowing, all powerful, all merciful compassionate gracious God who responds differently from day to day, rejoicing with us, grieving with us, but with a perfect knowledge and plan in all the problems we are going through in life. Jesus Christ is the same yesterday as he is today because yesterday is when Jesus Christ came to the world. Jesus Christ is same today as he was yesterday because today is where we have perfect relationship with him and gave our life. Jesus Christ is the same yesterday, today, and forever because Jesus Christ will be the same tomorrow as was yesterday and today because we cast all our hope on him. He is our hope of Glory. Jesus Christ of today must be the same as the Jesus Christ of yesterday; otherwise, we can never know Jesus Christ of today. Praise the Lord, we know Him and communicate with Him, through our prayer and supplication and through the Word of God that was written about Him in the history book of yesterday. Jesus Christ will never change, never go back on his word, his blessings never fail, nothing is impossible for him to do; he has the power and authority to solve all our problems and fulfill all our needs. He has the whole world in His hands.

The Son of God came to the world, he put on humanity; he became fully human and fully divine. All of God can be fully expressed in the human personality found in the Man, Jesus Christ; In Him the perfect revelation of God found embodiment. By his ascension he has been re-instated to the status of Son of God, which today is to Him by nature.

I will end this with a song writer that says: "Christ whose glory fills that skies, Christ, the true, the only light, sun of righteousness, arise, triumph over shades of night. Day spring from on high be near, Day star, in my heart appear. Visit then this soul of mine, pierce the gloom of sin and grief; fill me, radiance divine, scatter all my unbelief; more and more yourself display, shining to the perfect day." (Charles Wesley, 1743)

CHAPTER TWENTY-ONE

SANCTIFICATION, GLORIFICATION

United with Christ Jesus is to know our justification; it is declared righteous before God. When we are united with Christ, we automatically receive our sanctification. Justification is God declaring us righteous and sanctification is when God make us righteous, put in us an interest that we need to be placed in us that the two cannot be separated from the heart of believer of Christ. Both are connected in our Union with Christ, God declaring us righteous in his judicial action bound up with our death to sin. We see that to be justified by faith is to enter into a living union with Christ, to live Christ like justification by faith was a dynamic and creative experience of Apostle Paul as shown in his writing of the epistles. The righteousness, which God confers, is what God approved and expected from all believers. Therefore, in Christ Jesus we know who we are as a believer at the same time, in Christ we become what we become as a believer. Knowing Christ's justification and sanctification is edited by the spirit given to us.

Justification opens the way into a new life in Christ, while sanctification develops our new life in union with Christ by the power of the Holy Spirit. Therefore, we can say that salvation is in the sanctification of the Spirit of Christ; therefore, sanctification was achieved by the Spirit, which was given to us by Jesus Christ. Whereby, in union with Christ we become an adopted child of God into God's family we receive our inheritance, our sonship and His Sonship. All this happens by the gift of grace through faith, with divine initiative of grace, our response is by faith. Faith is now clearly seen as the foundation of salvation. Faith is the key-note of the Gospel subjectively as Jesus Christ is the objectivity of faith.

There are many facts about Jesus which the believers needs to know and understand that faith is a commitment on the basis of conviction, trust in Christ who is known to be worthy of our trust. Faith, therefore must be the conviction of the facts of the Gospel of God. For example, we are not justified by the works of the law, but by the faith of Jesus Christ. Sanctification and godliness means to be set apart for the work of the Lord. This means that we have been set apart and made holy in order to serve the Lord, or to serve the people of the world. especially Christians so that God will be able to achieves His purpose through them.

When we are sanctified, we are made holy for divine purpose of God that has been ordained before the foundation of the world. We cannot choose ourselves; God is the one that is doing the chosen. We cannot come to God by ourselves; He is the one that made us alive in Him. He breathed on us the breathe of life. We are in Christ therefore we belong to God the Father Almighty; we need to do what He call us to do on Earth.

A new life in Christ is to do what is pleasing in His sight. We have a desire to do good and live a life that God approves; a life that He wants His people to live. "How much more, then, will the blood of Christ, who through the eternal Spirit offered himself unblemished to God. Cleanse our consciences from acts that lead to death, so that we may serve the living God. For this reason Christ is the mediator of a new covenant, that those who are called may receive the promised eternal inheritance now that he has died as a ransom to set them free from the sins committed under the first covenant" (Hebrew 9:14-15).

"But if Christ is in you, your body is dead because of sin, yet your spirit is alive because of righteousness" (Roman 8:10), "I keep asking that the God of our Lord Jesus Christ, the glorious Father, may give you the Spirit of wisdom and revelation, so that you may know him better, I pray also that the eyes of your heart may be enlightened in order that you may know the hope to which he has called you, the riches of his glorious inheritance in the saints, and his incomparable great power for us who believe. That power is like the working of his mighty strength" (Ephesians 1:17-19), "But grow in the grace and knowledge of our Lord and Savior Jesus Christ to him be glory both now and forever Amen" (2nd Peter 3:18).

With all these Scriptures, justification means what happened to us is in the past, but we can apply it to the present. While sanctification means the believer is set apart to live and serve the Lord in any circumstances, in persecution or affliction, we must live enduring life in order to serve the Lord to the very end of our lives.

Glorification is after death, we live forever in happiness as children of God in Heaven. We will wake up in a new body; in a new life with all the children of God. The trumpet will blast, we will have a new body, a new mind, a new thought; we will go and meet the Lord in the air. "Blessed are they whose transgressions are forgiven, whose sins are covered. Blessed is the man whose sin the Lord will never count against him" (Roman 4:7-8). Justification involves the forgiveness of our past, present and future sins; God hold no longer our sin against us. God punished our Lord Jesus Christ for our sins. "Although they know God's righteous decree that those who do such things deserve death, they not only continue to do these very things but also approve of those who practice them" (Roman 1:32).

The Bible say that the works of the law no flesh will be justified in His sight. Making all the efforts to obey God's law reveal that we are a sinner, we need a Savior. God gave us the righteousness of Jesus Christ; He declares us righteous on the finished work of Jesus Christ. God imputes to us the righteousness of God in Christ. No one can earn justification by obeying the law, we cannot make ourselves good enough so that God will accept us, we cannot be saved by our own work. "Today salvation has come to this house, because this man, too, is a son of Abraham. For the Son of Man came to seek and to save what was lost" (Luke 19:9-10). We must look to Christ and Him alone for our righteousness and future happiness in order to be saved we must depend on Christ alone for our salvation not on our works.

There is no salvation in any other way, only through Jesus Christ's righteousness; Christ and Christ alone is the way to Heaven. "Jesus answered, I am the way and the truth and the life. No one comes to the Father except through me" (John 14:6). Christ is all-sufficient, and His sufficiency is what we need to be saved, receive Christ and you have eternal life, life everlasting. Our sanctification is the work of the Holy Spirit. The same Spirit which moved the prophets in the Old Testament, the same Spirit which is called the Spirit of Christ sanctifies the heart, mind and the body of all those who come to Christ so that they can be able to live a life that is acceptable in God's sight.

Sin will longer have dominion over them. The former manner of life whereby they are living in the flesh will be done away with permanently. Apostle Peter sees clearly that salvation is real, affecting the entire life of the believer in so many ways- in personal life and social life as well as in relationship with the husband and the wives and children. In the plan of God the Father, His purpose is the salvation through God the Son. This is connected with the work of Jesus Christ through His death, burial and resurrection; with His blood, He saved us. Received by faith in Jesus Christ to be conceived and revealed at the last day. Salvation with working in praises to God, in hope in the Lord Jesus Christ, in holiness, full of the Holy Spirit Power, in love therefore the love of God manifested in the heart and in spiritual growth with fullness of the Spirit.

God the Father is the source, God the Son is the procurer, God the Holy Spirit is the one by whom we are being sanctified. The Word of God is the cause of our salvation. The regenerating power of God resides in the Word of God. This means that the word of God is God, which live and abides forever. It is an inheritance into which it includes us and connects us to the blood of Jesus, which redeems us.

This is the incorruptible Word of God. We see the grace of God in the heart of people of the world as a tender plant in a strange and unkindly soil. We are the unkindly, unfriendly soil, which the Apostle needs to take off. Apostle Peter points out the grace of life, which means grace for living, he used grace by telling the husband to honor their wives as they will share with them in the grace of life in the future.

He also mentioned the grace of divine security which rests upon the divine call of God, which is also based on the foreknowledge of God, through the Spirit's sanctification and obedience and the atone blood of Jesus. From this Holy Trinity, God's grace is multiplied to us.

This divine security is the main purpose of power of good character. "But you are a chosen people, a royal priesthood, a holy nation, a people belonging to God, that you may declare the praises of him who called you out of darkness into his wonderful light" (1st Peter 2:9). We are to endure hardness in the guarantee of our victory. This blessing comes to us through the God of all grace and is seen in and secured through the sufferings of Jesus and the glory which will come to us. "It is written: I believed; therefore I have spoken with that same spirit of faith we also believe and therefore speak" (2nd Corinthians 4:13).

Justification by faith is God's action towards humanity in which we responded to God by faith. Faith and the Spirit are brought together in close relationship, whereby Apostle Paul preached about the spirit of faith, where he explained that it is God who gave every human being the measure of faith. He told the Corinthian believers that their faith does not stand in the wisdom of men, but in the power of God to salvation. The spirit received from God because he is the Spirit of God. Faith therefore, bestowed by the Spirit and on condition that believer receive the Spirit. Therefore, to have faith, and to have faith in God's gift in Christ is to be justified.

When the Holy Spirit dwells in our hearts we experience the divine Sonship and are adopted into the family of God. And all the blessings of the new relationship, peace, joy, liberty, are a guarantee to us by the Holy Spirit. The Christian life is in the Holy Spirit. All the things, which belong to our salvation, are made available to us in the Spirit and by the Holy Spirit. The Holy Spirit is the source of the entire believer's faith, as well as the agent of the believer's fruit. Whereby, love one of the important fruit of the Spirit, the supreme grace, comes from the gift of the Holy Spirit. Saving knowledge is one of the gifts of the Holy Spirit. It is by the power of the Holy Spirit Christian's live under the seal of the Holy Spirit that is secure until the day of redemption. We have to realize that the presence of the Holy Spirit in the church. The Spirit power from the creation, His fellowship to believers, the ministry of the Holy Spirit as God's ambassador under the Spirit controls. We are all baptized into one body of Christ.

The Holy Spirit is the principle of unity by which the whole community of believers is bound together in a common life in God; living for Him forever. The presence of the Holy Spirit increases our faith; our trust in God strengthened us in all the areas where we are weak. The presence of the Holy Spirit is loving unity in the fellowship of Christ. It is the Holy Spirit activity in human beings, which creates a new relationship with God and expressed as union with Christ. It is the same fellowship of the

Holy Spirit that humanity is sure through the grace of our Lord and Savior of the love of God.

This is an expository action of the Holy Spirit in the life of the believer and the community as well as the congregation. The Spirit's activity gave rise to new spiritual gifts within the church throughout history.   The Holy Spirit is the life-giving principal distributed through the body of Christ. It is by the Holy Spirit that believer's make his or her response to the Lordship of Jesus Christ as their Lord and Savior. The essential motive of all service for Jesus Christ and relationship within the fellowship of faith is love of God shed in abroad in our hearts by the Holy Spirit.

The Holy Spirit is related and in every aspect of our salvation to our justification, to our sanctification, our service and our glorification. We receive the Holy Spirit by faith as we become one by the Spirit into the body of Christ and the church.

We live as a Christian as we walk by the Spirit, through the Spirit we become a Christian and receive the grace of God in Christ by faith through the Holy Spirit. Therefore, the gospel of our salvation consisted and solely based and summarized as by grace in Christ, through the faith by the Holy Spirit. Therefore, the Holy Spirit's indwelling presence is the new in the history of this world, and it is the new experience for the people of God.

It is through the Spirit that we come to the newness of life, made a new man and a new creation. Believers in Christ are no longer in the flesh, but in the Spirit because of the indwelling of the Spirit of God in the hearts.

To be in Christ is to be made new through the Holy Spirit. Jesus Christ's work on Earth was done by the power of the Holy Spirit. The Spirit's activity in the humanity of Christ is evident. Jesus said that the work that He did, He was not the one doing the work; the Father did the work through Him. It is the same today with all the believers of Jesus Christ. The work that we are doing is not from us, the Spirit of Jesus who indwells in us is doing all the work through us.

The Holy Spirit's operations gave rise to new spiritual gifts within the church. The ground of salvation is the undeserved favor of the all-loving God who has taken the initiative on our behalf. Salvation is from the unlimited goodness and loving kindness of God. The divine offer of salvation therefore must be the human response; man must be willing to receive the gift of salvation.

CHAPTER TWENTY-TWO

CHRIST OUR HOPE OF GLORY

Those whom God effectually calls he also justified not by infusing righteousness into them, but by pardoning their sins, and by accounting and accepting their persons as righteous, not for anything wrought in them or done by them, but for Christ's sake alone; not by imputing faith itself as the act of believing, or any other evangelical obedience to them as their righteousness, but by imputing the obedience and satisfaction of Jesus Christ unto them; they receiving and resting on Him and His righteousness by faith, believers have no faith of their own; it is the gift of God to those who believed in Him (commentary on the Westminster Confession of Faith Chapter 11)

Faith, therefore, receives and rests on Jesus Christ and His righteousness as the main instrument of justification. Yet, it is not alone in the person justified, but is ever accompanied with other saving graces, and is not a dead faith, but works by the love of God in the heart. A those and only those whom God has effectually called He also freely justifies, that this is so proved according to the Bible: "And those he predestined, he also called; those he called, he also justified, those he justified, he also glorified" (Roman 8:30.) The truth is that God's calling and justification are both important as well as orders to salvation towards the steps in the God's execution of immutable and infallibly efficacious decree of election. The truth is that only those who believe are justified and only those who are regenerated can truly believe.

This justification is the act of God as the judge of all and the ruler of all. God's pardon of all sins of all the people on Earth, all the Christians and accounts accepts, and treats him as a person righteous in divine law. Justification is an act of God, whereby God declares on humanity those who believe in Him to be conformed to the image of His son. "What, then, shall we say in response to this? If God is for us who can be against us? He who did not spare his own Son, but gave him up for us all how will he not also, along with hi, graciously give us all things? Who will bring any charge against those whom God has chosen? It is God who justifies. Who is he that condemns? Christ Jesus, who died more than that, who was raised to life is at the right hand of God and is also interceding for us" (Roman 8:31-34).

CHAPTER TWENTY-THREE

THE GIFT OF GRACE

The covenant of grace in Christ Jesus is a treasury of merit grace, and thence we receive pardon and a new nature, we are free from the law of sting and death, free from guilt and the power of sin. We are now under covenant, the law of the spirit, the law that gives the spirit, spiritual life to quality us for eternal life. The foundation of this freedom is laid in Christ Jesus undertaking for us of whom He speaks.

When the law failed, God provided another method through His Son Jesus Christ who came to the world to do that which the law could not do. He took upon Him the nature, which was the corrupt nature of man.

Our salvation comes as a gift of God's grace and is appropriated by the response of faith. Faith in Jesus Christ is God's requirement for receiving His free gift of salvation. Faith is also what we believe about Jesus Christ, and the believer's heart response of trust that causes us to follow Him as our Lord and Savior.

The New Testament concept of faith clearly stated that faith means to firmly, strongly believe and trust in the Lord Jesus Christ and to maintain a personal relationship with Him. We must believe with all our hearts and with all our being by yielding our wills, commitment, our spirit, soul, body to Jesus Christ as he is revealed in the Scriptures.

Faith involves repentance; we must turn from our sin and put on Christ. Saving faith is always a repentant faith. "Godly sorrow brings repentance that leads to salvation and leaves no regret, but worldly sorrow brings death" (2nd Corinthians 7:10). There is a genuine sorrow for sin that leads to repentance, means when we have a change of heart that moved us to turn from sin to Christ, a repentance of turning from sin, from bad behavior, character or habits leads to salvation and brings glory to God. This is our responsibility as a believer of Jesus Christ to turn away from unholy things and begin to live a holy life.

Faith includes obedience to Jesus Christ and His words as to make our way of life inspired by our faith, by our gratitude to God by the regenerating work of the indwelling of the Holy Spirit. Obedience that comes from faith is the obedience that God approves; therefore, faith and obedience belong to each other. Both are inseparably together. At the same time: saving faith without our commitment to sanctification is not possible in the life of Christ believers.

Our faith must also include our personal devotion to the Lord Jesus Christ. We must glue ourselves to Christ, trust Him, loves Him, be thankful and be loyal to Him. True faith cannot be distinguished from love; it is part of our personal activity of our love and trust for our Savior.

We must practice the habit of self-giving by directing all our efforts towards Christ and His redeeming work. "But where sin increased, grace increased all the more, so that, just as sin reigned in death, so also grace might reign through righteousness to bring eternal life through Jesus Christ our Lord" (Roman 5:20-21).

Faith in Jesus Christ as our Lord is the act of a moment and continuing a life of growing and strengthening because we have faith in a specific person that die for our sin and rose for our justification. Our faith must become more and more great, our trust and obedience should be develop into loyalty and devotion, loyalty that will develop into an intense feeling of personal attachment to the love of Jesus Christ. This faith in God brings us into a new relationship with God and exempts us from the wrath of God. When we maintain a personal relationship with God we were automatically become dead to sin and alive in Jesus Christ through the indwelling power of the Holy Spirit.

God the Father revealed Himself as a God of grace who always showed loving kindness to His people not because they deserved it, but because it is in His attributes.

God desires to be merciful and faithful to His covenant promises made to Abraham Isaac and Jacob. Example of Passover: "Therefore, say to the Israelites: I am the Lord, and I will bring you out from under the yoke of the Egyptians. I will free you from being slaves to them, and I will redeem you with an out stretched arm and with mighty acts of judgment I will take you as my own people, and I will be your God. Then you will know that I am the Lord your God, who brought you out from under the yoke of the Egyptians. And I will bring you to the land I swore with uplifted hand to give to Abraham, to Isaac and Jacob. I will give it to you as a possession. I am the Lord" (Exodus 6:6-8).

Same in the New Testament, God emphasizes His grace in given us His one and only begotten Son on our behalf sinners.

God multiplied His grace to believers by the power of the Holy Spirit by imparting forgiveness, acceptance and power to do God's will, our services to him. God's grace manifests in all the areas of our life through the power of the indwelling of the Holy Spirit. All the work of redemption, the Christian life from the beginning to the end is based on the grace of God abounding more and more in the life of believers.

God's gift of grace spread to unbelievers so that they may be able to hear to Gospel preached, teach witness to them and as a result, they believe in Jesus Christ. God also gave the gift of grace to believers so that they can be set free from sin. Believers' are able to will and act according to the good purpose' believers' were able to pray and ask God for whatever they needed, believers' are obedience to God's commandments, believers' were able to grow in Christ and grow in sanctification. God's gift of grace enables the believers to witness for Jesus Christ in so many ways that are possible on this Earth more than anyone can imagine.

Believers' were able to humble themselves so that they can receive the gift of God's grace. Believers' desire, seek and diligently pray that the grace of God to abound more and more in their life. Believers' study the Bible, read the Bible, are the doer of the Word of God, and worship Christ and able to proclaim the Gospel of God through the gift of the grace of God. Believers' also fast, participate in the Lord Supper, are continually filled with the power of the Holy Spirit when they received the gift of grace. God's gift of grace is immeasurable and His grace abounds in the life of every believer of Christ.

Therefore, justification brings life for all believers, it becomes actualized in individuals as they believe in Christ and receives the gift of the grace of God's life and the gift of righteousness is through Jesus Christ by the grace of God.

If the salvation, justification and righteousness that God provides came by perfect obedience to the law, no one would be saved because no one has obeyed the law perfectly. But since it comes as a gift of grace received by faith, salvation may be experienced by all who respond to God, even the Atheist and the wicked. God in His infinite mercy mercifully forgives our sins and imparts divine grace by his Spirit and power to regenerate our lives and make us God's children through Jesus Christ.

Power, might, ability is part of character and attribute of God, it shows that God not only has the power, but also we can trust Him that he will accomplish His purposes and keep all His promises to us as he did to Abraham, the Father of many nations. "Therefore, since we have been justified through faith, we have peace with God through our Lord Jesus Christ, through whom we have gained access by faith into this grace in which we now stand. And we rejoice in the hope of the glory of God" (Roman 5:1-2).

CHAPTER TWENTY- FOUR

CONCLUSION SUMMARY

Justification by faith alone stated that we are sinners and faced the wrath of God; but God sent His Son to the world. Upon His account we were able to receive God's pardon, we receive unto us God's unending favor, we are declares or pronounced righteous and acquitted from all our guilt of sins. He removed the curse of Adam and Eve, and turns away from His wrath towards us. God gave believers right and blessed us with eternal life in Him. Because by one man's disobedience sin enter the world; and by one man's righteousness, the righteousness of Jesus Christ alone efficacious in the justification of us all. This is the righteousness of Christ, even His obedience, whereby in all things He fulfilled the will of His Father; as on the other hand, our unrighteousness is our disobedience and our transgression of the commandments of God.

The Bible says that: through the operation of God, there is a state where the constituted and united of our soul with Christ which is different from God's natural and providential concurs us with all the believer's spirit, as well as from all union of mere association, or sympathy, moral likeness, or moral influence, union of life, in the human spirit. While, most individual believers possess their personal distinctness, interpenetrated and energized by the spirit of Christ. The believer is made indissolubly one with Christ and becomes a member or partaker of regenerated, believing and justified humanity of which Christ is the head and the hope of glory. After we have been justified by faith and receive the gift of grace we are now become one with Christ, we are now ready to add work with our faith through our union with Christ. Which is maintaining a personal relationship with Him the risen, the ever living, the ascended our reserved omnipresent Lord Jesus Christ. Our union with Christ is the central truth of the Christian doctrine for all people in the universe. Our oneness with Christ is always at the ground of regeneration and justification.

Salvation is through the redemptive work of Christ, therefore, our oneness with Jesus is planned and directed, controlled by the Holy Spirit, which renewed and justified believers. We receive Christ atonement, God elects and call us the sinners begin in regeneration, which was completed in our conversion, declared justification, and approved in sanctification with perseverance. The blessing of oneness with Christ is the justification by faith. Justification brings or changes the believer's moral character, and begins or started in regeneration and completed through sanctification. When a sinner is born again, it will show in his faith hope in the Lord, love and he will live a holy life. Regeneration is completed with believer's repentance, faith, justification, sanctification and glorification. Most importantly this one life with Christ makes regeneration and all others things with it a great blessing.

It is life of Christ who joins Himself to us in order that we may join ourselves with Him and be one in Him as He and Father are one. The Holy Spirit is the principle master planner between the believer, God the Father and God the Son with the immeasurable power of the Holy Spirit. Christ gave Himself to those who love Him, to those who believe in Him with intimate personal relationship with Him. We see that regeneration and the work of the Holy Spirit in conversion cannot be separated. Only in Christ and through Christ a sinner becomes a new creature, justified. To be one in Christ begins immediately after our conversion. We are one in Christ, we are regenerated and justified both these two are the divine side of humanity, sinners turn only as God turns to him. God imparts life to man and man become a living being, the same happened in regeneration and conversion. If God did not makes us alive in Himself, pastors might be preaching from morning until night, the sinner will not turn, but as God made the sinner alive in Him, the sinner will immediately turn to God. This is the gift of the grace of God.

The majority of believers, as well as non-believers, always think that God is too far away from them. They don't believe that God the Son can live in their heart by His Spirit, but with the power of Christ's omnipresence and the power of the work of redemption, Christ is able to manifest His full presence in the life of individuals of those who believe in Him and with the power of the Holy Spirit sinners were able to receive the fullness of the Spirit of Christ, which is the Spirit of God. Jesus Christ is able to be with us in every place, in everywhere, in everything we are doing and about to do, in our home, work place and in the church.

Individual believers receive the fullness of Christ and Christ becomes the source of strength. The source of a believer's life pours from Christ into their lives because He is the source. Christians were able to confidently say Christ gives us great wisdom and in Him we can do anything because He cares for His children. This oneness is the source of our stability, once formed it cannot be dissoluble. There are many ties in the world that are always broken, but our oneness in Christ will endure forever, from this Earth to eternity.

The Spirit of God made us alive in Jesus Christ; Christ's life was imparted in us because He gave us His Spirit. By faith from first to the last minute believers will continue to live by faith, and in so doing they will be able to grow from one level of maturity to another. In this way, the believer will continue to make progresses along the path of righteousness in order to live a rich and full spiritual life in Jesus Christ our Lord. Faith alone and in Christ alone is forever and ever. Amen, amen, amen.

"And without faith it is impossible to please God, for whoever would approach him must believe that he exists and that he rewards those who seek him" (Hebrews 11:6).

There is no amount of good works that can compensate for lack of faith. Faith is not a feeling of strength; faith is the blessed assurance that my heavenly Father's Will is the best for me. And that He has my highest good is at the heart of every test. After all is said and done, when a man refuses to believe God, he is calling Him a liar. He who does not believe God has made Him a liar. Faith is not an astronomical strong viewpoint that stands enthusiastically and never hints a single person groaning in the middle of difficulties. Faith is focusing on Jesus Christ whenever my hope is fading away and I cannot find strength within myself to continue in the world.

Faith is like a synthetic mirror that hides a world of disappointment; Faith is claiming the brightness of the situation when we know quite well that there is trouble ahead. Faith is finding advanced reasons to be happy during trials and tribulations, drawing infinite love and power from Jesus who is the author and finisher of our faith, that is full of abounding and all sufficient grace. Faith is believing that all my pain and earthly problems will go away. Jesus Christ has a purpose by permitting what I am going through. Faith is hanging on holding on tightly to God's promise for me, meanwhile trusting whole heartedly in God's goodness in His wisdom and His power. Faith is to blindly believe that all things will be well. Faith is building on immovable truth, which cannot be revoked because it is clearly the written Word of God from the beginning of creation. Faith is believing that in all what I am going through God is always in control. Faith is placing our confidence in Jesus Christ's unfailing love and the awareness that Jesus is preparing us for our eternal home. Faith is battling with the realities of life seeking for peace in the world of violence, knowing that Christ is the answer to world peace because He defeated death on the cross. Faith is only in Christ alone; He defeated Satan and blesses us with eternal life. Faith is pretending that all our problems are gone because we put it in Christ hands. Faith is to believe that Christ is alive and very close to us; He controls the timing of our lives. It is faith in Jesus Christ alone that saves us and satisfies the requirement of justification by faith. Faith is placing all our fears, our struggles, focusing on Jesus, praying instead of worrying and crying. Faith is living confidently on God's knowledge and the indwelling power of the Holy Spirit. Faith is to seek God's favor of anointing, God's glory, love, God's Will and His joy in our lives. Faith is to accept all what is happening in our lives joyfully, observing that it is permissive order of God for us. Faith is to strive for the gold in everything we are doing, everyday of our lives. Faith is to pray and pray until the gate of Heaven is opened and Jesus Christ continues to pour out His blessing of answered prayer to us.

Faith is in Jesus Christ alone.

CLOSING PRAYERS

"May the God who gives endurance and encouragement give you a spirit of unity among yourselves as you follow Christ Jesus, so that with one heart and mouth you may glorify the God and Father of our Lord Jesus Christ. Accept one another, then, just as Christ accepted you, in order to bring praise to God" (Roman 15:5-7). I pray that the God of hope gives us hope in believing that we will be able by faith to totally surrender our life to the Lordship of Jesus Christ and the blessing of eternal life will be ours forever amen, amen, amen.

HYMN OF PRAISE

As the songwriter says: "For the beauty of the Earth, for the glory of the skies, for the love which from our birth over and around us lies. For the beauty of each hour of the day and of the night, hill and vale, and tree, and flower sun and moon and stars of light. For the joy of ear and eye, for the heart and mind's delight, for the mystic harmony linking sense to sound and sight. For the joy of human love, brother, sister, parent, child, friends on Earth and friends above, for all gentle thoughts and mild. For each perfect gift of thine to our race so freely given; graces human and divine, flowers of Earth and buds of Heaven. For the church that evermore lifted holy hands above, offering up on every shore her pure sacrifice of love. For thyself, best gift divine, to the world so freely given; for that great, great love of thine peace on Earth and joy in Heaven. Lord of all, to thee we raise this our hymn of grateful praise." Conrad Kocher, 1838, William H. Monk, 1861, Folliott S. Pierpont, 1864

BIBLIOGRAPHY

Matthew Henry's Commentary in One Volume Genesis to Revelation Edited by Re. Leslie F. Church, Zondervan Publishing House1961

Systematic Theology Church Last Things by Dr. Norman Geisler Publisher Bethany House 2005

John Wesley Study Bible Abingdon Press 2009

The Interpretation of Scripture by James D. Smart Westminster Press Philadelphia 1961

The Works of Jonathan Edwards volume I and II Yale University Press 2009

Charles Spurgeon Commenting & Commentaries Baker Book House Publisher 1981

John Calvin's Commentaries Series Baker House Publisher 2009

Martin Luther The Bondage of the Will, Create Space Publisher December 2009

D. L. Moody A Passion for Souls: by Lyle W. Dorsett Moody Publisher October 2003

John Macarthur Saved Without a Doubt David C. Cook Publisher March 2006

The Work of Thomas Goodwin Volume I of 12 Sovereign Grace Publishers Inc. January 2001

A. A. Hodge Westminster Confession A Commentary Banner of Truth Publisher June 2004

<u>BIBLICAL INDEXES</u>

Genesis: 12:1-3, 18:11-12, 25, 15:6, 4-5, 1:1-3

Exodus: 19:12, 24:8, 6, 7:4, 6, 6:6-8, 34:6-8

Leviticus: 9:8

Job: 13:18

Psalms: 27:1, 8:1, 62:1, 14:3, 130:3-4, 33:6, 8-9

Proverbs: 9:10

1st Samuel: 16:7

Isaiah: 25:6, 53:6, 3:13-14,

Ezekiel: 37:4-10

Micah: 7:18-20, 6:1-2

Habakkuk: 2:4

Matthew: 20:28, 7:18-20, 5:17, 20

Mark: 10:45, 1:4

Luke: 3:3, 19:9-10

John: 3:16, 14:16-23, 15:13-15, 6:35, 14:6-7

Acts: 4:12, 5:29

Romans: 5:20-21, 12:12-13, 3:1, 21, 5:1-5, 4:22-24, 8:14, 1:16, 2:29, 4:1-3, 5:10, 1:17, 5:19, 3:24, 5:1-2, 4:1b-2a, 3:15-16, 8:15,8:30, 8:31-34, 4:5, 8:10, 4:7-8, 1:32, 10:9

1st Corinthians: 6:19-20, 7:22-23, 2:4, 14

2nd Corinthians: 5:21, 4:7, 5:19, 7:10, 4:13, 17-18

Galatians: 3:25, 5:6

Ephesians: 2:10, 2:4-5, 1:5, 2:1-2, 1:17-19

Philippians: 3:9

Colossians: 1:21

1st Thessalonians: 4:13

Titus: 2:11, 3:8

Philemon: 1:17-19

Hebrews: 7:25, 9:14-15, 11:1-3

James: 2:14-16, 2:24-26, 2:17-18, 1:3-7, 2; 21,

1st Peter: 2:9-10

2nd Peter: 3:18

1st John: 2:15-17

Revelation: 2:7, 19:22, 22:17

BENEDICTION

"The grace of our Lord Jesus Christ, the love of God, and the communion of the Holy Ghost, be with you all" (2 Cor. 13:14).

Amen, amen, amen.

MAY GOD BE GLORIFIED FOR THE GREAT THINGS HE HAS DONE IN OUR WORLD.

Books previously Published by the author

Grace Dola Balogun by

Grace Religious Books Publishing & Distributors, Inc.

PRAYER THE SOURCE OF STRENGTH FOR LIFE - English Edition

Prayer the Source of Strength for Life is a powerful book that will energize your spirit to pray more and more until the prayer is part of your life and until the Gate of heaven is opened and your prayer is answered. Your prayer life will change your life.

LA ORACION FUENTE DE FORTALEZA PARA LA VIDA - Spanish Edition.

Dios nos dio el poder de la oracion, quiere que lo usemos; debemos illamar, comunicarnos con el en todo lo que estemos pasando. El espera saber de nosotros.

Spirit Power Volume I and II both discuss the power of the Holy Spirit in the life of believers

The Power of the Spirit of God begins from the creation of the world up until today. That power will also continue until Christ returns to reign. Hallelujah!

THE CROSS AND THE CRUCIFIXION

Our Lord Jesus Christ died on the Cross to bring forth love and compassion. Sin's impact on human life brings all other evil into our world, from one society to another society, from one culture to another.

But in Christ, we are clothed with His holiness. We have the gift of eternal life. The gate of heaven is open and we are eligible for our inheritance in heaven.

Hallelujah! Hosanna in the Highest. Jesus Christ paid it all, unto Him all we owe. The Cross of Christ is the Cross of joy, peace, and righteousness to all who believe in Him.

THREE SOLUTIONS FOR WORLD PEACE

This book will help people to find a solution to world peace even though many religions are promoting different interpretations of God. Reading this book will enlighten your heart to the three-word solution that can change hatred, violence, jealousy and wickedness into love. Evil will turn to good. Even tribalistc war and civil war, it will turn wars between nations into peace. Practicing this solution for one year will change the entire people of this world; they will look for good in each other. This book is an eye opener to the people through awareness of who God is in the world and in individual lives.